SHADOWY CORNERS

CATHERINE OSBORN

SHORT STORIES
OF
MYSTERY, MENACE AND HUMOUR

Published by New Generation Publishing in 2022

Copyright © Catherine Osborn 2022

First Edition

The author asserts the moral right under the Copyright, Designs and Patents Act 1988 to be identified as the author of this work.

All Rights reserved. No part of this publication may be reproduced, stored in a retrieval system or transmitted, in any form or by any means without the prior consent of the author, nor be otherwise circulated in any form of binding or cover other than that which it is published and without a similar condition being imposed on the subsequent purchaser.

ISBN   978-1-80369-515-0

www.newgeneration-publishing.com

New Generation Publishing

By the same author

For Adults:

Call me `Your Ladyship' – *The Secret History of a Rhondda Girl*

Sweet and Sour – *Light Verse edged with Darkness*

Shadowy Corners – *Short Stories of Mystery, Menace and Humour*

For children:

Behind the Attic Door

The Image of Jonathan Plum and other Stories

The Monster of Hagstone Hall

About the Author

Catherine, Lady Osborn was born in Wales, but lived most of her adult life in London. She has had a varied career as a schoolteacher, actor, model for book jackets, and charity worker for Voluntary Service Overseas.

She is now retired and lives in a small flat near Regents Park during which time she has written five children's novels, this collection of short stories, a book of Light Verse, and a lively autobiography: `Call me `Your Ladyship'. Several of her short stories have appeared in magazines or won prizes in competitions.

She has been married twice and widowed twice, with one daughter who is an illustrator of children's books, and two granddaughters.

Besides writing, she enjoys reading, current affairs, amateur dramatics and going for walks in London's wonderful parks and gardens.

SHADOWY CORNERS

CONTENTS

TALES OF MENACE 1
  Windbreak 3
  Beware The Sandman 13
  Family Honour 24
  A Passion For Tidiness 32
  A Hell Of A Night 40
  Deadly Intruder 50
  The Foster Child 56
  Celebrity 68
  A Perfect Gentleman 75
  Obsessed 84
  Hocus-Pocus 92

FAMILY MATTERS 101
  The Porcelain Dancer 103
  Fatherly Feelings 111
  Replay 119
  Omission Of Truth 127
  A Question Of Degree 137
  Waiting For Polly 146
  Talking To Maggie 154
  The Last Goodbye 160

TIME TO SMILE 169
  A Box Of Chalks 171
  Getting Rid Of Gladys 179
  Plum Pudding 188
  The Black Porcelain Horse 198
  Dejeuner Sur L'herbe 204

The Piano Teacher 212
Dropping Out 220
The Chocoholic... 226
Haitian Ritual – 1981 233
Dressed For The Occasion................................. 239

TALES OF MENACE

Revenge, jealousy, greed and unjust laws, mingle with malign, supernatural forces in these chilling, twist-in-the-tale stories

WINDBREAK

We call them the *quarrellers,* the pair who've arrived, uninvited, at *Windbreak* and wandered about in its garden.

It was our little girl, Jenny, who gave them that name, for it was she who first met them.

It was late July. We'd been settled in *Windbreak* no more than a year when she came running into the kitchen from the garden. "Mummy, there's people sitting on the seat behind the rose bush." She pulled at my elbow, a frown crinkling her forehead. "Are they visitors?"

"I doubt it." I wiped my hands on a kitchen-towel and followed her into the garden.

"They're horrid," she whispered. "They keep quarrelling, and the man made the lady cry. I said 'hullo', but they didn't even look at me. That's rude, isn't it, Mummy?"

As we hurried down the path I thought I heard snatches of conversation, but it might have been the rustle of leaves or the buzzing of insects, for when we reached the love-seat behind the rose-bush, it was empty.

"They're gone," Jenny murmured. She must have noticed my sceptical look for she tossed back her tangle of curls and stuck out her chin. "They *were* here. I didn't make it up. And the man was horrible. His voice was all growly. And he had a fuzzy beard and glasses, and a face just like this." She screwed up her eyes and twisted her mouth into a scowl.

I didn't pay much attention. Tourists, I thought, unable to resist a peep at our garden. Or maybe Jenny imagined them. She's an only child, sometimes lonely and dreaming up companions. She's done it before.

I forgot the incident until, a week later, she came running up the path once more, breathless with anxiety. "Come quick, Mummy! Those *quarrellers* are here again, and that awful man is hitting the lady and hurting her. Make him stop!"

Once again I followed Jenny, but once again, there was no sign of them. I began to wonder if we should take her to a psychiatrist.

My husband, Richard, rolled his eyes at the idea. "Honestly, Kate, the child's fine. She's got a lively imagination, that's all. Probably seen something on TV that's sparked it off."

I wasn't so sure. I kept a close eye on her after that. It's not too difficult now I've given up my job in town.

For a week we heard nothing more of the *quarrellers*. She's forgotten them, I thought.

But one day, on opening the kitchen window – it was still very hot – I heard voices wafting in from the garden.

I looked out but could see nothing.

Jenny joined me at the window. "It's the *quarrellers*," she whispered. "The man's being horrible to his wife again."

She climbed onto the chair below the window and leaned out. "Look, here they come."

This time, I saw them. First, the woman, pale, willowy, with blonde, fly-away hair, emerging from behind the trees at the bottom of the garden. And she was running, as if for her life.

Behind her appeared the shadowy figure of a man, fists clenched, mouth set in an ugly line. "Helen, come back here!" he shouted. They were both coming up the pathway, towards the house. As they got closer, I could see that the man had a beard and black-rimmed glasses.

I felt my blood pressure rising. Who were these people? How dare they invade our garden?

I opened the window wider. They had reached the patio now.

"Would you mind telling me what you're doing here?" I yelled. "This happens to be private property."

Neither gave me as much as a glance.

Instead, the woman turned her anxious face to the man behind her and gasped out, "I was only going to see Sarah, George. Please don't hurt me."

"Lying bitch! You were seeing *him* again, that fellow you met at the conference, the `kind gentleman', who gave you a lift home. And I thought that's all there was to it." He spun her round to face him. "But I was wrong, wasn't I? You slept with the bastard!"

"No, George, no! You're mistaken." She twisted away, eyes desperately seeking escape.

"You were *seen*, damn you!" He pulled her back by the shoulders and shook her. "And you're still screwing around with him. I should have guessed the truth when I met him myself, and saw the way he looked at you."

He flung her forward. She went sprawling, hitting her head on the patio.

I rushed to the kitchen door, ready to give him hell. "You maniac! I'll report you to the police!"

I hurried down the steps. I'd invite the woman in, give her a cup of tea. Whatever had happened, she didn't deserve to be pushed around like that.

The patio was empty.

I stared, not believing. Where had they gone?

I ran through the gate leading to the outside lane, the parched earth hard beneath my feet, a stray thorn stinging my ankle.

No sign of them. No sound even. Only the crackling of twigs as a squirrel bolted up a nearby tree. And the buzz of a mosquito flying into my face.

I shook it off and stood, gazing into the emptiness, listening to the silence. Who *were* these people?

I longed to talk to Richard, but he was away on business. I didn't want to worry him.

Over the next few days, I kept Jenny close to me. We avoided the garden. The plants got watered, but that was all.

On the day before Richard's return, I went up to our bedroom to change the sheets. I paused outside the door, a prickle of fear starting up at the back of my neck. Someone was in there. I could hear the sounds of drawers being opened and shut.

I was about to turn and run to the phone, when I heard a sob from inside. I made myself open the door.

And then I saw her, that same woman I had seen in the garden. She was alone and had a suitcase open on the bed. Her eyes darted about furtively as she hurried to fill it.

She appeared to be taking clothes from the wardrobe, but they were not *my* clothes. They were shirt-neck blouses and pleated skirts, things I never wear. Her forehead was creased with lines of nervousness, and from time to time she scurried to the window and peered out before continuing her task.

I stepped into the room. It was as if some unseen force was pushing me forward. "Who are you?" I murmured. I moved closer and peered into the porcelain-like face.

She didn't answer, seemed not to see me.

I stretched out a hand to touch her. At the same moment, she and the suitcase on the bed blurred and melted into the blue and white stillness of the bedroom.

Shaking, I closed the door and went downstairs. My teeth were chattering in spite of the August heat. Had it been a hallucination? Or was I witnessing the unthinkable: the souls of dead people who had once lived here?

I thanked heaven Richard was due back soon. The whole thing was making my head ache and I was beginning to jump at shadows.

The following day, while reading to Jenny in the sitting-room, I heard footsteps in the passage outside. I was ready to burst with relief.

"Richard?" I hurried into the passage.

There was no answer, but I heard a door slam.

Jenny ran past me towards the study. "Daddy, daddy! You're back," she yelled.

She pushed open the study door. I took her hand and followed her inside.

A shadow appeared to move in the corner. I froze. Jenny let out a cry.

It was not Richard. It was the intruder, George.

I stood inside the door, transfixed, my daughter's hand clasped tightly in mine. I wanted to turn tail and run, pulling Jenny after me, but I felt paralyzed, glued to the floor. I could only watch.

He was standing beside the writing-desk, holding something in his hand. It looked like a pill-bottle. He was fingering it, turning it round and round and muttering, "So, she's leaving me for *him*? I'll see her in hell first."

"It's that *quarreller* man," Jenny murmured. "Why is he here, Mummy?" She began to whimper and flatten herself against my waist. "I don't like this house anymore." The whimper turned to a howl, the howl to an outburst of noisy sobs.

I came to myself then, and hurried her into the sitting-room. It had a lock on the door so I locked us in, knowing at the same time that locked doors are no protection from spirits. I prayed that my husband would return soon.

He arrived an hour later. I rushed into his arms, half-sobbing in relief, my words tumbling out in a torrent of incoherence. "Oh, Richard, thank goodness you're back! We've got to leave this place. At once. There are ghosts. And one of them's really evil. Please, let's go away. Now."

"Ssh!" He put his arm round me, but I saw his face darken. "We're not moving, Kate," he said, when I'd calmed down. "I'm not going through all that again."

"But don't you understand? We can't cope any more. The place is haunted." I broke into another fit of sobs.

He shook me. "That's nonsense, Kate! Stop it! Get a grip on yourself!"

I turned away, tight-lipped. He'd change his mind. I'd make him. If he didn't, I'd leave, and take Jenny with me. Perhaps then he'd come to his senses.

As we sat in the kitchen that night, drinking tea, I tried once more to discuss moving house, but Richard seemed preoccupied, too lost in his own thoughts to listen. His eyes had a far-away look. His lips smiled at something invisible.

Then I heard it: the noise outside the window. It was a strange, irregular sound, like something being dragged from the patio to the lawn.

"What was that?" I sat up, alert.

"What? I didn't hear anything." Richard lost his glazed look and frowned.

"I thought … Oh, never mind. It was probably nothing."

He relaxed, leaned back in his chair, and began to chat about the business deals he'd made that week.

I tried to focus, but was too on edge, and too busy trying to make out another sound outside. It came again.

"Listen! Do you hear it?"

It sounded like a distant wail.

Richard paused. "Cats," he said, decisively. "Cats from next door."

"Please, I'm worried. Let's take a look."

We went outside. Moonlight flooded the garden, covering everything in a veil of translucent gauze. It looked calm, beautiful. The scents of honeysuckle and jasmine drifted on the night breeze. We walked down the path towards the love-seat, then on to the lily-pond. Everything was still, silent. But as we neared the pond, we heard a choking, spluttering sound and a splash of water.

I started. Richard gripped my hand and we ran through the ornamental arch till we could see the pond before us. And there, beneath the moon, we saw a sight that made us cry out: the heavy shape of a man bent over something that kicked and struggled at the side of the pond. As we got closer, we could see it was a woman. He was pinning her to the ground with his body and thrusting her head into the water. She was writhing and twitching. But by the time we reached the place, the twitching had stopped.

"What the hell?" Richard raced towards him. "You bastard! Kate, get the police!"

My husband's a big man, sure of his strength. He made a grab for the killer.

"It's no use, Richard," I called out. "They're not real."

Too late. Richard stretched out his hands and, as he did so, killer and victim began to fade away, until both had vanished into the night air.

Richard stood gaping at his empty hands, while I, beside him, tried to stop shuddering. What did this violence mean? Surely if it was something that once happened here, we would have heard about it?

Whatever it was, Richard changed his mind about staying. The next day, he put the house on the market. The day after, he arranged to take time off work, and we went to stay with friends and to search for a new house.

Today, we are back at Windbreak, but only to see the estate agent. He is bringing our buyers with him. They viewed the place while we were away and agreed the asking price. Now they are coming to measure up and decide where their furniture will go.

I'm feeling guilty. Poor devils! But perhaps they won't be harassed by the *quarrellers* as we were. Maybe the spirits, or whatever they are, will leave them alone.

Richard reads the paper while we wait. Jenny is busy with her colouring-book, sticking out her tongue as she concentrates. I potter, feeling calmer now. We all are. Two days ago, we saw a house we liked and put in an offer. It's been accepted.

The estate-agent arrives early, our buyers close behind him.

I go to greet them with a smile. But my smile freezes. The man is thick-set with a beard. He wears black-rimmed glasses. The woman is pale, willowy, dressed in a pleated skirt.

"Let me introduce you to George and Helen Leech," the estate agent says.

Richard steps forward, an arm outstretched in welcome. He has never met the pair in daylight, so there's no sign of alarm on his face. But I see something else there, a kind of joy, that only adds to my disquiet.

The woman flashes him a smile of recognition. "So *you're* the vendor?" She turns to her husband. "George, this is the kind gentleman who gave me a lift from the conference that time. Isn't it amazing?"

My heart turns to a lump of ice.

She and Richard exchange glances, private, heavy with secrets.

George, her husband, purses his lips. "Amazing indeed," he grunts.

The words sound unreal as if coming from a distant planet, or a dream. I try to speak but can only gaze at the couple in silence.

Then Jenny looks up from her colouring book and gazes at them too.

I see her face change, a frown appear between her eyes and her mouth open like a letter 'o' as she lets out scream of terror.

BEWARE THE SANDMAN

He should never have told Eddy about the Sandman. Not at the tea-table in front of Claire and his mother. It was asking for trouble.

"Alex! Stop frightening Eddy with that ghastly story! You know how nervous he is." His mother glared at him, eyes glittering dangerously, as she reached for the milk-jug.

"Yes, cool it, you sadistic little pig," Claire piped up. "You're nearly eleven and ought to know better. Eddy's only six."

Alex sniffed. Anyone would think he'd put arsenic in his brother's tea. He pulled his best *Quasimodo* face at Claire, while his mother wasn't looking, and mouthed the words 'Drop dead!' He loathed his bossy sister. She was always having a go at him.

He sneaked a glance at Eddy and smirked when he saw the frightened look on his face. Little wimp! He loathed *him* too. He didn't know why. Perhaps it was that lock of blonde hair that flopped over his forehead, like a girl's, his whiny voice that brought the others rushing to his attention, or the turquoise-blue eyes that everyone went so dotty about.

It was partly on account of those eyes that Alex told him the Sandman story, and told it with such relish. Simon Hicks, a boy in his class, had a video of it at home, and they'd watched it together, goose bumps multiplying as the grim story unfolded.

It was a legend from Eastern Europe, so Simon said. According to the legend, the Sandman wasn't some nice, cosy old-timer, who throws sand in children's eyes to help them sleep. Oh no. He was a creepy, shadowy fellow who sat in wait for a child to drop off, then gauged out his eyes and made off with them to some remote island.

"Yuk!" Alex murmured, when the film had ended. "That was really gross."

Nevertheless, he couldn't wait to inflict Eddy with the grisly details. He wanted to see his eyes widen, like a scared rabbit's, his plump hands fly to his face, his shoulders tremble.

Eddy didn't disappoint him. He shook with terror at the story, and late that night, awoke with a shriek as the Sandman slipped through the window of his dreams and settled itself on his bedside chair. Still yelling and screaming, Eddy scrambled out of bed and flew to his parents' room.

The night after, he was too afraid to go to bed at all.

"Don't be silly, darling, there's nothing in your bedroom to be afraid of," his mother said. "You had a bad dream, that's all. Probably due to that cheese-omelette we had for supper."

"I'll get you a night-light," his father said.

Eddy's moan turned to a shriek. "N-o-ooo! Then I'll *see* him."

His parents exchanged anxious looks.

"He can come in with me," Claire said.

"No, Claire. You've got exams coming up. You need your sleep." Her mother smiled coaxingly at Eddy. "Come now, lambkin. You must learn to sleep on your own. Leave your door open, then you can call out to us, if you wake up, frightened."

His father added more words of comfort. "Tell you what, Eddy, I'll read you a *Thomas the Tank-Engine* story and stay with you till you go to sleep."

Eddy's face crumpled. "That's no good. That's what he's waiting for, for me to go to sleep."

Alex stifled a giggle. He'd scared the kid gutless. Better not tease him any more, though. If he were caught at it again, there'd be murder. For all that, he couldn't resist sidling up to him afterwards and saying in a low, rasping voice, "The Sandman's coming tonight, Eddy, so you'd better take care ..."

Eddy stuck his fingers in his ears, his face screwed up with fear. "Stop it, Alex, stop it! I'm not listening."

Alex hopped about, holding his stomach and almost losing his breath with laughing. His kid-brother's face! Those bulging eyes! They were enough to make you curl up.

He felt a thump between his shoulder-blades. He spun round. It was Claire. "*I* heard you," she barked. "Shut up, and leave your brother alone!"

He did, for a short while. Claire was sixteen and a lot bigger than he was. She could slap really hard, if she wanted.

But directly her back was turned and Eddy had taken his fingers from his ears, Alex carried on teasing. "... Soon as you're asleep, he'll squeeze out your eyes. And there'll be blood everywhere, all down your face, and over the bed.

And you won't be able to scream for help because you'll be *paralyzed*. And you won't be able to see, because your eyes have gone and ..."

He broke off. Footsteps. And there she was again, his rotten sister, all ready with her fisticuffs. He jumped back and spread out his hands in front of him to fend her off.

"You hit me once more and I'm telling our dad."

"Go on then. And when I tell him *why* you got a thump, he'll give you another one."

"No he won't." Alex pushed past her and ran off, calling behind him, "Fatty four-eyes! Lump of lard!"

She ignored him, settling her glasses tighter on her nose and getting the Ludo out to play with Eddy.

Alex made his way to the stairs. He'd have a go at that new computer-game in his bedroom. Half-way up, he heard Eddy's high, whiny voice calling from below. "You better watch out, Alex. The Sandman might come after *you* tonight, instead of me."

Alex gave a guffaw of laughter. "Dummy! There's no such thing. I was having you on. It's just a story."

"No it isn't. I've seen him. And he's horrible. He's got a rod-thing for pulling your eyes out. And he smells like dead fish."

Alex frowned. "You're making it up. Little liar! It's a story, I tell you."

He wandered to his room. A cold splinter of fear rose up in his stomach. He remembered, from the video, that rod-like weapon in the Sandman's hand. They called it the *Extractor*. He was sure he hadn't told Eddy about it.

The murky details of the film went round and round in his head, making it hard to focus on his new computer-game. At last, he banged his fist on the table and gave up.

Stupid story!

It was the same when he tried to sleep that night. Images from the film flew into his mind: the boy in his dressing-gown, climbing the wooden staircase at dusk, candle in hand; the dark figure emerging from the window-curtains and shuffling towards the bed ...

He wriggled further under the sheets. Get a grip! he told himself. It's a story. A daft old fairy-story. He turned over and tried to think of cheerful things like the goal he'd scored at football that morning.

Then he heard a noise. A creak on the landing and another on the stair. He went rigid, almost forgetting to breathe. At last, hand trembling, he felt for the light-switch. Slowly, he uncovered his face and looked around.

Relief swept over him. Everything as it should be. Computer-table in the corner, videos on the shelf, Harry Kane, the football star, smiling at him from the poster, opposite. He began to breathe again. Idiot! It was probably someone getting up for the loo.

He edged himself to the side of the bed. Better make sure though.

He got up, tiptoed to the landing and glanced outside. Empty. He crept towards his brother's room and peeped through the half-open door. That's when he let out a shriek.

There was someone or something huddled in the bedside chair. A second later, he was aware of a sudden movement, a rush of air, as a shadow flitted across the room, followed by a rumbling at the window. Shaking from head to toe, Alex switched on the light.

The bedroom was empty.

Not only was there no intruder. Eddy had vanished from his bed.

He heard footsteps, then his father's hoarse whisper behind him. "Alex, what's happened? Was that you I heard screaming?"

"Eddy's gone," Alex faltered, pointing to the empty bed.

His father shrugged. "Gone to the bathroom, I expect, or to get a drink."

"Dad, I thought I saw someone sitting on that chair …" He looked at it again. That's when he noticed the buff-coloured quilt draped over it. He bit his lip. Daft twit! So that's what he'd seen.

They heard a noise from downstairs, like a cupboard being banged shut.

"That'll be Eddy. Back to bed now, Alex."

Alex hung over the banister, watching his father go downstairs. He heard Eddy cry out, "I'm not going back to bed, Daddy, I'm not. The Sandman's on my chair again. He's waiting for me to go to sleep."

Alex grinned. That quilt had fooled them both. Odd though, the feeling he'd had of someone moving about. What if …? His grin faded. Better take another look. Once again, he stepped into Eddy's bedroom, carefully scanning every corner. Finally, he pulled aside the window-curtains. Nothing. He went limp with relief.

He was about to move away when, glancing down at the window-sill, he spotted an irregular patch of pale yellow. He inspected it closely. Sand. He could smell something too. Seaweed? No. Couldn't be. They didn't live anywhere near the sea.

When he went down to breakfast next morning, he could hear Eddy in the kitchen, banging his spoon on the table and shouting, "It's not a nightmare, it's not. It's the Sandman. He said he's going to nick my eyes, unless …"

Alex saw his mother fling up her hands. "Eddy, darling, it's just a horrible made-up story. And your brother deserves a good smack for telling it to you."

She looked daggers at Alex as he came in and seated himself at the table.

Alex made one of his astonished-at-such-injustice looks, mouth open, eyebrows disappearing under his thatch of hair. "How was I to know he'd be such a baby and believe it all?" He gave a snort. "Afraid of the Sandman! What a gook!"

"That's enough, Son." His father eyed him, sternly. "Eddy's still an infant, remember."

Alex, anxious to avoid another lecture, softened his voice. "It was that quilt over your chair that frightened you, Eddy. It must have looked a bit spooky in the dark."

"No. It *wasn't* the quilt," Eddy wailed. "It was *me* what put that there. I throwed it over him so I wouldn't see his scary face. Then I runned out."

His father attempted a chuckle. "He can't be very fierce if he lets you do that to him."

"He *is* fierce." Eddy dropped his spoon with a clatter. "Only he ain't supposed to touch you till you go to sleep." Tears started to fall. "N-n-nobody b-believes me."

Alex rolled his eyes as his mother hurried over to comfort him. "Of course we do, sweetheart. We'll see Dr Scott this afternoon. He'll give you something to get rid of your nightmares."

"They're *not* nightmares, and I don't *want* to see Dr Scott." Eddy kicked the table-leg then, looking plaintively at his mother, said, "What I want is to change rooms with Alex tonight. I'll be all right then. It'll all stop."

Claire, who had just come in and was busy at the toaster, turned to Alex. "Well, how about it, tough guy? It was you who started it all. Why not help your little brother out?"

Alex nearly choked on his mug of tea. "You must be joking. I got all my video games and stuff in there. I don't want Eddy messing about with them."

"Don't worry," Claire said, quickly. "I'll help you move them out. Or is it that you're *scared*?" She sniggered as she sat down and began to butter her toast.

Alex felt he would explode. "Me? Scared of a stupid Sandman? Don't make me laugh!" He glowered at Claire. She went on sniggering.

Maddened, he threw down his toast. "Okay, we'll change rooms." He wagged a finger at Eddy sitting opposite. "But it's only for tonight, remember. Your cupboard is too small for all my stuff. Anyway, it's a kid's room. I don't want wallpaper with teddy-bears all over it."

His mother heaved a sigh of relief. "That's settled then." She leaned towards Eddy and stroked his hair. "Happier now, lambkin?"

Eddy brightened. "Oh yes, Mummy. I'll be all right in Alex's room." He smiled sweetly at his brother. "Thank you, Alex. I hope you like sleeping in my bed."

There was something sly about that smile, Alex thought. As if he were gloating at getting his own way again. He finished his toast and got up. Still, it's only for tonight. He scraped back his chair. And there's nothing to be afraid of. Absolutely nothing.

He climbed upstairs to collect his schoolbag. When he came to Eddy's room he paused. His heartbeat began to quicken. There was still the matter of that sand.

He went in and hurried to the window-sill. It had gone. Vanished. Perhaps, he thought, it was never there in the first place. Perhaps he'd imagined it. Just as he'd imagined that weird shadow flitting about.

Feeling calmer, he fetched his schoolbag from his bedroom and ran downstairs.

That night, Claire helped him shift his things into his brother's room. "Eddy's a real pain," Alex grumbled. "I told him it was only a story."

He spoke briskly, trying to ignore the squiggly feeling starting up in his stomach. He wished he hadn't offered to sleep in Eddy's room. But he couldn't get out of it now. They'd think he was afraid. And there was nothing to be afraid of, was there?

It was already dark when he finally yielded to pressure and trundled up to bed. He switched on the light in his brother's room and hovered at the door a moment, chewing his lip. "Better check things first," he muttered. He bent down and stole a quick glance under the bed, looked carefully in the wardrobe, then hurried to the window to peer behind the curtains …

He halted, frowning. He was being ridiculous. What was he scared of? Only little kids were scared. Kids like Eddy, who imagined things. Goofy things. Like a Sandman in the bedroom.

He climbed into bed and picked up a comic from the bedside chest. He'd brought in a pile of his favourite ones.

He began to read. An hour passed. He heard Claire thumping up the stairs and into her bedroom, then his mother.

He went on reading. Before long, however, his eyelids began to grow stiff, and the pictures in his comic blur. Soon, the comic dropped from his hands His eyes closed.

His father, the last to go to bed, noticed the light on under his door. He went in, switched it off and went out again, shutting the door quietly behind him.

It was the middle of the night when Alex awoke. At first, he didn't know where he was. And then he remembered. He was in his brother's bed. He remembered, too, his brother smiling at him, mockingly from his dream. And his words, "You'd better watch out, Alex. The Sandman might get *you*, tonight, instead of me."

A cold, creepy feeling came over him. Fear. And as his fear mounted, the room seemed to grow colder. He shut his eyes and snuggled down under the bedclothes, shutting out the room and the cold. But not the fear.

He dropped off again into an uneasy sleep. And then he heard it. A kind of rumbling at the window, followed by the creaking of floorboards. And after that, a snorting, slithering sound, as though someone or something was dragging itself across the floor towards his bed. And with it came a smell, a sickening smell that made him think of dead, decaying fish and seaweed washed up on the beach. As the slithering came closer, he began to hear harsh, shuddering breaths and feel them cold against his face.

The creature, whatever it was, settled itself on the chair beside the bed.

From behind closed eyelids Alex saw it clasping something long and steely in its hands, something with a ring at the end. The Extractor.

It was the Sandman, and it was going to take out his eyes. Not knowing if he were asleep or awake, he opened his mouth to scream. But no sound came. He tried to struggle from his brother's bed. But he couldn't move.

The Sandman rose with a ghastly smile, bent over its victim and lowered the Extractor onto his face.

The following morning, Claire awoke to the wailing of an ambulance drawing up outside. She rushed downstairs. Her father was in the hall, going to the door.

Hurrying into the kitchen, she found her mother weeping quietly, Alex on her lap.

Eddy was close beside her, reading a story.

"Mum, what's happened?"

Her mother let out a sob.

"Claire, is that you?" came Alex's voice, weakly.

"Of course it's me, Alex. Open your eyes."

His eyelids fluttered open. She let out a scream. His eyes had gone, leaving his eye-sockets empty, gelatinous holes.

"We don't know what happened," her mother said, between sobs. "Some psycho …"

Eddy looked up from his book. "No, Mummy. It was the *Sandman*. I told you. But don't cry, 'cos he won't get *me*." He snuggled up against her. "Now he's got Alex's eyes, he'll leave mine alone. He promised."

They turned to stare at him, aghast.

But Eddy, an angelic smile on his face, flicked over the pages of his book, and didn't notice.

FAMILY HONOUR

This story is based on a true event which occurred in Saudi Arabia towards the end of the last century. The parents, however, and what happens to them are fictionalised.

Things appear to be changing in Saudi Arabia, and women's lives becoming easier but at that time, they had very little freedom or power. They were not allowed to drive, or to travel without a male escort. Punishments for fornication or adultery were dictated by Sharia law and were unbelievably harsh by Western standards.

My brother, Kahlil, nudges my elbow, as we stand in the heat and dust of the town square. "Come away, Nura, this is no place for a woman."

I sweat under my black *abaaya*. It's the middle of May, already hot, with few palm trees here for shelter. In June, my husband, Abdul, will drive us to the mountains of Taif to escape the heat of Riyadh. I once looked forward to it. But not anymore. My heart is too full of grief.

Kahlil lays a hand on my shoulder, his eyes pleading. "It'll be a rough business, Nura. Think about it. They'll drag her in, shackled, and force her to her knees while the mob looks on and taunts." He lifts his eyebrows. "You can cope with that, you, her mother?"

I feel a great lump rise to my throat and stick there. "I want just one glance at her face," I murmur. "One last glance at my beautiful Sara, before …"

I swallow, my words choked in despair.

My brother's eyes glisten with sympathy. He is a kind man. Beneath that wiry beard and massive frame, he's gentle and caring, not arrogant or scornful of women, like so many Saudi men. But he's not Saudi. He's Kuwaiti, like me. It was good of him to drive me here today.

But he's shuffling his feet now, anxious to go. "Why upset yourself further?" he argues. "Why not grieve at home, with Abdul?"

I taste bitterness in my mouth. "With Abdul? With my husband? Why do you think he refused to bring me here himself today?" My voice hardens. "Because he's choking on his guilt, that's why. Because it was he who demanded her execution. His own daughter."

A flame of anger shoots up inside me. "Even if she were guilty, the penalty is flogging, not stoning. But Abdul's not content with that. He's like a maddened bull and insists on death. `For the family honour,' he shouts, thumping the table. And the *mutawa* support him for his moral convictions."

I give a snort. "Moral convictions? The child's *innocent*. Even Abdul must realise that by now. But he can't lose face. He must defend the family honour." I spit out the words.

I see a flicker of doubt cross my brother's face. "Right or wrong Nura, they found her *guilty* in the Shari'a court." He sighs and stretches out his arms. "Think, she had sex with five young men! Begged them for it, they said. If that's true, it's shocking – a crime of *Hudud*. Knowing Abdul's temper, I wonder he didn't kill her himself. Odds on he'd have got away with it."

"Or served a paltry six month sentence," I say with a bitter laugh. "After all, what's a child's life compared with family honour? As for those young louts, what punishment do they get? A lecture from

Father, with their promise not to do it again?" I hear my voice grow shrill. "Those boys *raped* her, while the rest of us were away. They were high on drugs, smuggled in from abroad, no doubt. And your nephew, Hadi, after promising to protect her, did nothing."

Khalil frowns and hisses in my ear "You're shouting, Nura. Calm down."

"Calm down? How can I? They raped her, Khalil and made her pregnant. Took away her marriage prospects, her future. Begging for sex? She was thirteen. She'd only just been veiled. She knew nothing about such things."

Lines of doubt linger on his forehead. "How do you know they were taking drugs?"

"Jane told us, our Filipino maid. She caught them with American magazines too – you can guess the sort – then found Sara crying and screaming."

My voice trembles at the memory. I bite my lip till it bleeds. "You know the rest – the hospital visit, the phone call to the police, the *lies* ..."

My stomach churns. "The boys denied everything, of course. Hid their drugs. Had their story all prepared. And Abdul believed them, as did the court. Who would take a woman's word against a man's?"

Kahlil shakes his head. "I still don't see there's any proof of *rape*."

I click my tongue. What do I expect? Men stick up for each other, even a man like Kahlil. There must be witnesses to rape. A woman's word counts for nothing.

Disappointed with Khalil, I push him away. "Don't touch me. You'll have the *mutawa* arresting us for lewdness."

I glance around me. Noon prayers are over, and more people are joining the crowd, restless, impatient for spectacle, getting angry in the hot sun. They are mostly men, young thugs, laughing, jostling each other, keen for the fun to begin. I see older men too, stern-faced men of Allah. But some of them, I know, take trips abroad and buy girls of ten or eleven for their pleasure, paying their parents a few riyals for the privilege.

And here they are, ready to punish my daughter for fornication. They'll seize the largest stones from the pile, and push forward to the front, so they can meet their aim with ease. I'm told it can take two hours before it ends.

A stirring in the crowd disrupts my thoughts. The truck has appeared, with men emptying rocks and stones in a pile. I shut my eyes. My brother was right. I should never have come. But I have to see my child. Who else will show her support? I want to give a sign of my belief in her, hold out my hands in compassion. Then I will find some quiet corner and pray to Allah to punish those who sent her to her death.

I shiver in the heat as I remember that she gave birth just hours ago. A girl. The *mutawa* and police will be guarding the ward's entrance, so no one can help her escape. Bound and shackled, she'll be brought here to die, still weak from giving birth.

And the time is come. My heart plunges to my stomach as I see a police car arrive at the square and grind to a halt. The crowd moves forward, curious, eager. Trembling, I watch the police officers pull my child from the car and drag her to the far end of the square.

"Let's go. You've seen enough." Kahlil taps my shoulder.

I pay no heed. I throw out my arms and push my way to the front. "Sara, my child," I gasp.

I see her shackled, unveiled, her head drooped over her chest. She looks half-dead as they force her to her knees on the ground.

I move my lips in desperate prayer. "Oh, Allah, the Compassionate, the Merciful, save my poor, innocent daughter! And punish those who sent her to her death!"

I lift my veil. It is forbidden, but I must see clearly my child's face. Those close by nudge each other, titter and peer at me. I don't care. Let them. Let the *mutawa* come and arrest me.

"Cover your face, woman," someone in the crowd hisses.

My brother comes and clutches at my elbow. "Nura, Nura, the *mutawa* are watching."

"To hell with the *mutawa*!" I push further forward. "Sara. Look up, Sara, I'm here, with you. See." I stretch out my arms.

I believe she hears me. She lifts her head. I see her lips move, the pleading, the terror in her eyes. At last, she looks at me, a dead, despairing look.

I wring my hands, my eyes stung with tears. I feel her pain, her fear, her helplessness before this mob. Yet, I can do nothing. My breath comes out in deep, gulping sobs as I fall forward to the front of the crowd.

The men there shove me back. "Where's this woman's husband?" one demands. Another yells into my face, "Stop screeching, woman. The girl's a whore. She deserves all she gets."

I face them, fists clenched, their voices almost drowned out by the pounding in my head. I become a wild creature, ready to spit and claw at their faces. "She's no whore," I scream. "Leave her be, you ruffians, you low-born dogs!"

They gape at me and back away, astonished at my insolence. But at this moment, I don't care what I say, or do. Let them kill me, if they must.

Before more damage can be done, Kahlil charges over and grabs my arm.

I take one last look at my daughter's face, before they place a gag in her mouth and fasten the hood around her head. Then I drop my veil and turn away.

Suddenly, my rage is spent. A deadly calm sweeps over me.

I hear a man call for quiet. He reads out Sara's crime then announces the start of the execution. There is a rush to the pile of stones. Khalil tries to drag me away, but I shake him off. There is one more thing I have to do.

Sweat and dust fill my nostrils as I elbow my way through the crowd pushing towards the pile of stones. I choose a jagged piece of rock and hide it under my *abaaya*. It feels rough and unrelenting in my hands. That done, I hasten with my brother towards the car park.

My mind is made up. When we get home, I shall carry the rock to the marriage-bed and slide it under the sheets. "Sleep with that, Abdul," I'll say, "for I'll never come to your bed again. That stone is like my heart, as hard and cold as my wifely love." Later, I shall leave him and go to my mother in Kuwait. I know where the passports are kept. And I know how to forge my husband's signature for the letter of permission I'll need to travel. I shan't miss him or my spoilt, shiftless son. I renounce them both.

We arrive. I thank Khalil for his support and walk through the iron gates into my husband's house. I want to relieve myself of the heavy stone, but I'm startled by a noise coming from Abdul's study. I stop to listen, then make my way there.

The door is ajar. And there is Abdul, slumped over his desk, hands resting on his head. A bottle of whisky, from the black market stands, half-empty, beside him. He is letting out drunken, snorting sobs.

My mouth hangs open. A twinge of pity touches my heart. "Abdul, you are grieving about Sara?"

He looks up, stupefied. "About Sara? My shameless daughter?" He slaps his hand on the desk. "No!" His voice breaks. "It's my son I grieve for, my Hadi."

"Hadi?"

"Yes. Hadi. The police found him, with drugs in his pocket. I can't believe it. He'll go to prison, or get eighty lashes." He lays his head on the desk. "Oh my son, my treasured son." His shoulders heave under silent sobs. "How can I renounce my son?"

"You renounced your daughter. Where were your tears for *her*?" I feel again that flame of fury shooting up inside me. He has not a grain of pity to spare his daughter.

I think of her dying in the square, despair in her eyes, the cruel gag forced into her mouth. I see again the jeering youths, thrusting their hands into the pile of stones, hear them laughing and yelling in my face.

The mental picture reminds me of the rock I'm holding under my *abaaya*.

Like one in a trance, I draw it out, step behind Abdul and, with all my strength, bring it crashing down on his head. He utters a cry. A spasm passes between his shoulder-blades. I pay no heed, but strike again and again, until the skull cracks and the blood spurts out -

- Until he is still, and there is silence.

Then, calm again, I place the stone beside his body, go to the telephone, and call the police.

A PASSION FOR TIDINESS

This story is set in England in the 1960s, a time when many families, if they were not too hard up, started going abroad for their holidays, often on package tours to places like Spain or Italy. The typical holiday of the past at the English seaside lost its charm for a number of people and became unfashionable.

Rick Verner glanced out at the lead-coloured sea and the blanket of clouds brooding over it. "Perfect," he murmured.

He turned to help his wife onto the boat while the boatman waded into the water to give it a shove.

Amy Verner, having brushed the boat-seat with a tissue, planted her plump behind upon it, then watched in chilly silence as her husband fitted the oars into the rowlocks and began to pull.

"You're raving mad!" she burst out at last. "You heard what the boatman said. There's a storm coming."

"Not for ages," Rick assured her. "Come on, Amy, lighten up! A boat-trip will make a nice change. Your friend, Chloe, thought it was a great idea."

"Oh, *her*!" Amy gave a snort. "She's always siding with you these days. I don't know what's come over her."

Rick chuckled to himself. *He* knew well enough. It was becoming painfully clear that their holiday landlady, the buck-toothed Chloe, was beginning to fancy him. He was appalled rather than flattered by the discovery. Yet, he had to admit that Chloe's inflamed passion had its uses. Without her help this morning, he could never have persuaded Amy to take part in this venture.

"It's ridiculous boating at all this time of year," she grumbled. "If you'd only get yourself a half-decent job, we could take our holidays in the summer. Not wait for the cheap rates in the autumn."

And if you weren't such a mean bitch, expecting *me* to pay for everything, he thought, we could be sunning ourselves in Ibiza or Tenerife, like everyone else, instead of shivering on the English coast year after year at your friend, Chloe's crummy guest-house.

Aloud, he said, "Are you comfortable, dear?"

Resting on his oars a moment, he took a bag of toffees from his pocket and passed it to her after picking out one for himself. He dropped the wrapping on the floor of the boat. Hastily, almost guiltily, he picked it up again and put it into his pocket before she could rebuke him.

A place for everything and everything in its place. That was one of Amy's golden rules. As he pulled steadily away from the shore he reflected that it was her passion for tidiness more than anything else that had been the decisive factor in this whole enterprise. More decisive even than her building-society savings which she would never touch, no matter how hard-pressed they were. Nearly fifty thousand pounds and, God knows, they could do with it.

But it wasn't the money so much. It was living in a house where an easy-going man could never relax. The sharp, never-ending "Richard, did you leave this here?" "Richard, why can't you put things away when you've finished with them?" Nineteen years of it. He'd had enough.

"Aren't we going rather a long way out?" A troubled frown creased Amy's forehead.

"Not at all, dear. Appearances are deceptive at sea."

He hid a smile, fully aware that they were approaching a turbulent stretch of water. Boating accidents here were not uncommon.

A sudden flutter of nervousness rose to his throat. There would be an inquest. Awkward questions. He rested on his oars again, keenly alert to the rising wind and darkening sky.

The sea was a deep and sullen green, stained here and there with patches of purple. Rick shivered. It would be cold in the water. But it wouldn't be for long. From the shore they'd soon see the capsizing boat and come to the rescue. Lucky that he was a strong swimmer and that Amy couldn't swim at all.

His nervousness subsided. It was all in the bag – the end of nagging and miserable penny-pinching, the beginning of the road to freedom. Boldly, he grasped the oars and rowed forward.

A sudden gust of wind hit the boat on the beam and she heeled. Amy clung to the gunwale in dismay, causing the heeling motion to grow into a turbulent rolling. This was the moment.

Rick stooped down and heaved the bung out of the bottom.

"Those policemen had no right to question you when you were in a state of shock." The little red-haired nurse frowned as she plumped up her patient's pillows.

"They were only doing their duty, Nurse." Rick heaved a melancholy sigh.

"Your landlady came and took your wet things away to dry. I hope that was okay?"

The nurse picked up her tray and moved to the door. Then, on a sudden impulse, she turned and said, "You'll get over it, Mr Verner. Time is a great healer."

Rick gave a grief-stricken attempt at a smile. The nurse went out, eyes glistening with kindly tears.

Alone at last, he relaxed. A smile began to play at the corners of his mouth and before long his whole body was shaking with silent laughter. He had done it. Finally done it.

It hadn't been easy. In those angry waters, Amy grew wild in her desperation to stay alive. Seeing the boat sinking and the oars floating away, she had clung to Rick, struggling frantically, almost drawing him under with her. But as she swallowed more and more water and became steadily weaker, her vice-like grip on him relaxed until he was finally able to shake himself free.

The police officers had listened sympathetically to his story.

"It was terrible but, you see, I was half-drowned myself. In the end, I just had to let her go."

His tone of voice, Rick recalled, had been just right. Broken with emotion at suitable points, it was, in the main, tight-clipped and brave but mingled with a dreary numbness. It was clear that the officers were satisfied with his account.

Of course, when they recovered the boat, they'd notice the bung was missing. Still, he had a plausible answer up his sleeve. It was probably loose already, he'd say, and the rough water had forced it out.

Anyway, soon as probate was over, he'd buzz off to South America, maybe shack up with some gorgeous senorita there. The future was full of possibilities.

Later that day, Chloe came bustling into his room, oozing concern and maternal tenderness. She had brought his brief case together with a basket of fruit.

"You poor, poor boy! What you've been through!"

She lowered her squat form into the bedside chair and grasped his hand.

Rick stifled the impulse to snatch it away. He could afford to indulge her. After all, once everything was over, he need never see the hideous old fool again.

Chloe sat silent a moment, resting her toad-like eyes on his face. At last, in a tone deeply earnest, she said, "It's terrible that Amy's dead, I know. But *you're* alive, and you must think of your future."

"I've got no future," Rick said, slipping into his voice of weary resignation.

"Of course you have." She smiled a toothy smile. "It's early days yet, but in time, you'll find plenty of women only too proud to be the second Mrs Verner." She lowered her eye lashes coyly. "I know I would."

Repelled, he shook his hand free of her grasp.

"It's what Amy would have wanted," she insisted, voice like treacle. "Besides …" She gave him a knowing look. "You feel the same about me. No use denying it. A woman can tell these things."

Rick stared at her, stupefied.

"It's too soon yet," she went on, gazing thoughtfully at her plump hands, "but in a few months time, when everything's over …"

Rick shuddered. "You'd better go, Chloe," he said,

"You're making a fool of yourself. And your timing's terrible." He paused, then added with a tremor, "Amy and I might have had our little differences, but for all that, I – I loved her."

"Really?" She narrowed her eyes. "Is that why you threatened only two days ago to shut her up for good and all?"

He shrugged. "We all say things in temper that we don't really mean."

"Perhaps. Pity though that others heard. Things like that have a habit of getting around."

There was a dangerous edge to the soft tones. Rick stirred restlessly beneath the sheets. Perhaps it wasn't a good thing to make an enemy of Chloe. She knew nothing, of course, apart from the state of his marriage. Still …

He leaned over for his briefcase, took out his cheque book and wrote out a cheque for two thousand pounds. If there was one thing about Chloe he was sure of, it was her love of money.

"Look here, you've been a good friend to Amy over the years," he said, genially. "I'm sure she'd have wanted you to have a little something to cheer you up in these sad circumstances."

He pressed the cheque into her palm.

"You're sure it won't put you in the red?" She gave a smirk. "But then, it won't be for long, will it? You'll soon get Amy's building society money, *and* the cash from her policy." The bulging eyes were alight with greed. "Took the policy out three months ago so Amy said. Pity about that." She frowned. "Bad timing. Makes the accident look sort of planned."

"What are you driving at? That it wasn't an accident?"

She was after more money, damn her! Well, she wouldn't get it. "You haven't a shred of real evidence."

"Perhaps not. However …" She paused and gave him a confidential wink, "while I was going through your wet pockets, I found this." She clicked open her handbag.

Then, with the air of a conjurer taking a rabbit from a hat, she pulled out an object which she waved triumphantly before him. "The police will be so curious to know why, in such a crisis, you took out the boat's bung and put it in your pocket."

He stiffened. His throat went dry.

"You can deny it, of course. But then, besides everything else, there's the little matter of the cheque. To keep me quiet, perhaps?" She cocked her head to one side and gave him a girlish smile. But there was no disguising the threat in her voice. "I'd better report it, hadn't I?"

She rose and leered down at him.

Rick tried to calm the pounding of his heart. It was all circumstantial, he told himself, the weather warning, his threats to Amy, the policy, even the boat-bung … There was no real proof.

Nevertheless, with a clever prosecutor …

"No, don't report it," he said at last.

Bitterly, he waved goodbye to hopes of a tranquil future. A habit of tidiness drummed into him over nineteen years had ruined such hopes, ending with the pocketing of that boat bung.

He glared at the buck-toothed Chloe with a hatred fierce and indestructible. The thought of spending the rest of his life with her appalled him.

But he'd find a way out.

He wondered if *she* could swim.

A HELL OF A NIGHT

Cassie shivered as she hurried along Woodley Way. It was a hell of a night to be walking home. Rain spattered down from a moonless sky, and a chill Autumn wind blew in her face, forcing her long blonde hair to stream out behind her.

She wished now she'd taken Mrs Bloom's advice and got a cab. "A young girl like you shouldn't be walking home this time of night," Mrs B had argued, "not with a killer on the loose. You'll end up like that schoolgirl, Caroline West, found dead in Woodley End Woods last month. And that other one a couple of months before. Be a good girl now and let me call a cab." She reached for the phone.

Cassie jumped up. No way. She wasn't going to dip into her baby-sitting money to pay for a taxi. Not when she was saving for a smart-phone. She picked up her money, popped it in her little red purse and made for the door. "I'll be okay," she called behind her. "Cheers." And she was off.

She didn't feel so brave now. The road was dark, deserted. The wind seemed to bite right into her, tearing at her jacket, pulling at her hair, flinging loose twigs and dead leaves from the wayside trees onto her shoulders. She shook them off and pulled her anorak tighter around her. Two miles to go. She hurried on, her footsteps echoing through the empty street.

She paused to brush another leaf from her face. The sound of footsteps went on. Tap-tap, tap-tap.

A cold splinter of fear rose up in her stomach. There was someone coming along behind her.

She glanced over her shoulder.

And saw from the light of a lamp post some twenty yards behind, a thin, gangly figure with hunched shoulders. He walked with a roll, from side to side, as if drunk. Then she saw him stretch out an arm and wave it up and down, as if gesturing her to stop.

She jerked her head away. She knew someone with a walk like that. Someone from her year in school, a real scary guy called Joe Bumford, the last person a girl would want to meet on a dark night! At school, with the rest of the gang, she didn't give a toss. There, they laughed at him, yelled out `Bum-face' and imitated his walk. Sometimes they grabbed his schoolbag and hid it. It was hilarious.

But out here, on her own, and on a night like this, it didn't seem funny any more. Especially after yesterday. That's when they went too far. They taunted him about his father, calling him a `schizo'. He almost exploded. Then she and Mike tripped him up. Sent him flying over a heap of stones. Everybody laughed like crazy. But when he got up, blood trickling from his lip, hissing something through clenched teeth, the laughter stopped. There was a look of menace on his face, a threat that sent a tremor of fear up her spine.

She quickened her pace. She was sure it was him following her. And he was out for revenge. He must have heard about her baby-sitting job with the Blooms in Essex Street. Perhaps he'd been hanging around outside, waiting.

A gust of wind blew an old paper bag into her face. She swore and pushed it away. The footsteps behind grew louder. And closer. She gritted her teeth and broke into a trot. Her stalker did the same.

He started shouting something too. But when she tried to catch the words, the wind tossed them away, emptying them of meaning. All she could hear with clarity was the shuddering of leaves and her heart pounding in her ears.

"Please God," she gasped into the wind.

And straight away, a miracle. A beam of light from an approaching car which slowed down and ground to a halt beside her. Then the door opening, and a woman's voice oozing comfort and motherly concern. "Hop in, love. You're being followed. I'll take you home."

She was well-built and bosomy with greying hair and plump, benevolent face.

Breathing a long sigh of relief, Cassie sank down on the seat beside her.

"Thanks," she murmured. "I live in Tooley Lane."

The woman frowned. "That's nearly two miles away. What you doing, a young girl like you, walking all that way alone, on a night like this? Won't your mum be worried?"

Cassie shrugged. "She won't mind. She's too busy with Morris, her new boy-friend."

"Well, I'd worry if I were her. What's your name, love, and how old are you? You must be still at school."

"The name's Cassandra. I'm sixteen. And, yeh, I'm still at school. St George's."

"Hm. I thought so," she said softly, nodding her head. "And who was that fellow behind you, I wonder?"

"Oh, some jerk from school, who's got it in for me."

"He didn't look like a *schoolboy*. And what do you mean, got it in for you?"

Cassie relaxed and took a piece of chewing-gum from her pocket. She's a nice old girl, she thought, a real Mum-type. She felt she could tell her anything, even the truth, and it would be okay. "The thing is," she began, "me and my friends made fun of him, calling him names and that. Then yesterday, one of us tripped him up and sent him flying."

"That wasn't very nice. Why did you do that?"

Cassie shrugged. "Dunno, really. Only he's so creepy-looking and has this hooked nose, like a beak. And a funny, slouchy walk." She demonstrated, rolling her shoulders from side to side against the back of the car-seat. "It was only a bit of fun."

The woman made no comment. Cassie fiddled with her scarf and changed the subject.

"I usually get a lift home after baby-sitting, but there was something wrong with the car."

"Couldn't you have got a taxi?"

"Can't afford it. I'm saving all I get for a smart-phone."

The woman paused, then said slowly "Well, dear, I might be able to help you there."

Cassie stopped chewing a moment. Her eyes widened. "You could? How?"

"We've got a spare one at home. Top of the range, I believe. If it suits, you're welcome to it."

Cassie gasped. Was this for real? "But don't you want it yourself?" she asked.

The woman laughed. "I'm useless with machines," she said, "and my husband has his own phone." She sighed. "The spare one belonged to our daughter."

"Doesn't she want it any more?"

The woman gave a sad smile. "Not anymore. She died last year, poor love."

Her voice trembled as she went on. "She was about your age. Perhaps you knew her. Angela, her name was, Angela Dorking."

Cassie spat the chewing-gum out of her mouth and stuck it hastily into her pocket. She hated talking about dead people. "I might have known her. Slightly," she answered.

"Well, what's past is past." The woman heaved another sigh then turned the corner into Woodley End. "This is where I live. Come in and I'll get you the phone."

"Great!" The old girl was an angel. Cassie was glad now she hadn't got that cab.

She followed her in.

A tiny hall led into a sitting-room with brown leather sofa and matching chairs. A photograph of a stubby –looking girl with bobbed hair hung on the wall. Angela. Cassie turned away. At the far end of the room was a door. The woman walked towards it and flung it open. Then she called through: "Come on up, Robert. I've got someone to see you."

Cassie heard a distant grunt then footsteps climbing up. He padded into the room in slippers, not a tall man, but powerfully-built, with wiry hair and eyes that darted about.

The woman looked at him, eagerly. "Her name's Cassandra, Robert. Ring any bells?"

"Cassandra?" He puckered up his forehead. "I'm not sure." He had a low, rasping voice.

"Oh, you must be sure, dear. Really sure this time. Take a good look. She goes to St George's School, just like our Angela did. Same age too. And she's …" She moved towards him and whispered something. He nodded slowly. Cassie shrugged. Why the hell should he know her? She didn't know him from Adam.

"Hm. Cassandra." He was giving her the once-over now, looking her up and down with those darting eyes. "Hair's right," he muttered, "Long and blonde. Hm. Interesting." His eyes seemed to glaze over as though he were engrossed in his thoughts.

Cassie turned her head away, sharply. Stupid old git! Hadn't he seen long, blonde hair before! She rolled her eyes. Perhaps he had a thing about hair. Ah well, let him go on staring. She'd put up with a lot more to get hold of that phone.

She forced a smile. "I'm told you've got a smart-phone going spare," she said.

He emerged from his reverie to give his wife a questioning look. She returned it with a nod.

"Ah, yes. We keep it in the basement. Let me find it first. Then you can come down and have a look at it." He went through the door again, and down the stairs.

"He'll only be a minute, dear. You want a cup of tea? You must be cold."

"No thanks." Cassie felt a tingle of excitement. She'd never dreamed she would get a top of the range smart phone. And for free. Now all that money she'd saved could be spent on other things. Like those trainers she'd seen the other day that her measly mother would never buy her, any more than she'd buy her a new phone. She felt her face glow. But now… What a marvellous night this was turning out to be!

A hoarse call rose up from the basement.

"It'll be ready for you now, dear." The woman ushered her to the doorway. "You go down first. I'll follow. Watch the stairs. They're a bit narrow. I wouldn't want you to fall."

Cassie clambered down and found herself in a dimly lit workroom. It smelt of sawdust and paint. A workbench stood opposite the stairs with shelves above it, filled with tools.

She looked for signs of the smart-phone, but saw nothing. "Well, where is it?" she asked.

The man stood motionless in front of his workbench, arms folded. He didn't answer.

"Well?" She stared at him, impatient, eyebrows raised in question.

He met her stare in silence. Then his mouth stretched into a smile. Thin and icy.

Behind her, at the top of the stairs, the woman was shutting the basement door. She came down, crossed over to her husband, and stood beside him. Cassie hadn't realised quite how big she was. Her shoulders were broad and strong, her hips massive. "I think first, dear, we must have a little chat." Her voice was soft as velvet, but she no longer smiled.

"What do you mean? You said you were going to show me a smart-phone." What the hell were they up to? It was getting on for twelve. A bit late for chats.

"I know, dear, but we must talk first." She turned to the man. "What do you think, Robert? Is she definitely the one?"

He pursed his lips. "She's the one all right."

"You're sure now? Absolutely sure? We mustn't make another mistake. Like the last time, and the time before."

"She's the one, I tell you. I remember her now."

"I thought she was," the woman said quietly. She let out a long sigh of satisfaction. "She'll be the last then. After that, we can rest and forget it all." She felt for his hand and squeezed it.

"Just a minute. What's with you two? What the hell are you on about?" She wanted to scream with frustration. There was no smart-phone. They'd been lying, fooling around with her. She might as well go.

She turned and started up the stairs. "If you haven't got a phone for me, you're wasting my bloody time. I'm going," she yelled behind her.

She grabbed the door handle. Twisted it, turned it.

"It's no use, dear, it's locked."

"Then you can bloody well unlock it. I'm going home."

Tears of rage and disappointment welled up in her eyes, followed by a prickle of fear. She began to thump and kick at the door.

The man let out a snarl. "Come back down, you little bitch! You're not going anywhere."

A smile distorted his face as he saw her stumbling down the stairs. He began to mock her, putting on a falsetto voice, high and squeaky. "Loser!" he jeered. "Tramp! Retard!"

She gaped at him. The man was mad. Raving bonkers.

His wife lifted her eyebrows. "Why so surprised? Aren't they the names you called our girl when you and your pack chased her down the road each day, demanding her dinner-money, making her life a misery." Her voice hardened. "Didn't you do the same to her that you did to that poor boy you told me about tonight?"

The man, his face dark with menace, lumbered towards the stairs where Cassie stood at the bottom. She backed away. Her heart began to pound. They were loonies. Both of them. "Let me out!" she squeaked. "You're talking a load of rubbish. I didn't know your daughter."

"Stop lying!" His voice began to shake. "Do you know what happened to our girl because of your bullying?" He paused, his eyes boring into her. "She hanged herself, that's what she did." His voice rose to a shriek. "And she was fifteen years old."

With hands of steel he grasped Cassie by her shoulders and dragged her to an alcove at the side of the stairs. "And that's what we're going to do to you," he growled. "Look up at the ceiling, Cassandra, there on your left!" He pointed upwards.

Cassie, her teeth chattering with terror now, looked up. It was then that she saw the dangling rope with the noose at the end.

"That's where she died, dear," the woman said. "It's the same rope."

Cassie sank to the floor, a quivering mass of jelly, whimpering, crying, pleading. But she knew it was no use. They were going to kill her. And there was nothing she could do to stop them.

Outside, about a mile away, the thin, gangly man with slouched shoulders trudged on, buffeted by the wind and the rain. He glanced again at the red purse in his hand and shrugged. "Ah, well," he muttered. "I did try to catch her up after she dropped it. But she took no notice."

He shook his head. Then that car had come and in she hopped. Hadn't anyone told her she shouldn't take lifts from strangers, especially with a killer on the loose? Kids! He clicked his tongue. Didn't they teach them anything these days?

He sighed, turned up his collar, and stuck the purse in his pocket. He began to whistle. Nearly home. And thank goodness. It was a hell of a night.

DEADLY INTRUDER

There was no doubt about it. My front door was unlocked, even open a crack. Yet, I remembered clearly locking it that morning before leaving for work. I paused on the step, ripples of unease starting up in my stomach.

Someone had been in my apartment. Was there still perhaps, going through my papers, messing up my clothes, tampering with my computer ... A burglar?

Perhaps. I ran my tongue pensively along my lips as I reached for the door-knob.

No one else had a key. Except Mike. And it wouldn't be him. He never saw me these days. Too wrapped up in that woman, Laura. Mooning about her. Even now, weeks after her muddied corpse had been dragged from the Thames, riddled with bullets.

Autumn wind whipped through my hair. I shuddered and loosened my grip on the door-knob. An unsettling thought struck me. Suppose it was *her* in there? Laura? On another of her visits.

I stood, glued to the step, obsessed by the thought. It sounds crazy, I know, but she's been here before, I swear it. Not her body, of course, but her spirit, drifting from room to room, poisoning the air with her damned scent, sniggering, playing games. I've heard her, felt her. Again and again

I could feel her now.

Dread clutched at my throat. With an effort, I shook it off, thrust my keys in my pocket, and plunged into the hallway.

There, the heaviness of her presence grew stronger. I could feel once again her ghostly breath fanning my face. Laura. Dead yet not dead.

Either that or my mind was playing tricks on me.

Get a grip! I told myself. The dead can't hurt you. The dead can't do anything.

I straightened, flung open the living-room door and flicked on the light switch.

Mother of God! The place was a tip. Cups and drinking-glasses smashed on the floor, next to the upturned coffee-table. A vase broken on the dresser. Potted plants flung from sills and ledges, scattering earth and flowers onto the carpet. Drawers and cupboard-doors gaping open.

My head began to swim. A ghost? Unlocking doors? Trashing my apartment? Absurd! It had to be a burglar. Some damn thief, after money, no doubt, and my collection of DVDs. Annoying but hardly unusual in this part of London.

I wanted to laugh with relief. Better a burglar than a ghost. I'd go and find out what was missing. Then I'd clear up the mess, put everything away. I'm the orderly type. I can't stand my place in a shambles.

I set the coffee-table upright and propped my briefcase on the top. As I rose, I caught sight of my face in the mirror above the fireplace. I groaned. What the hell had happened to me? My skin looked blotchy, coarse, my eyes bloodshot. I'd let myself go since Mike left me for that bitch, Laura.

I turned away, a bitter taste in my mouth. One shouldn't speak ill of the dead, I know, but that woman was poison. And her death had done me no favours. Mike spurned my love still, even my efforts to comfort him. When they'd first got together, he said to me, "We can stay friends, can't we, Honey-bun? Pop round and see us, whenever you like. Laura won't mind."

I did, for a while. I thought I might win him back. Some hope. As soon as she found out the truth about us, that we'd been more than just `friends', her manner towards me changed. She began to abuse and torment me, like a cat with a mouse.

Ah well, water under the bridge. She couldn't torment me now. I glanced around at the open drawers, the smashed crockery. I'd soon sort it out. Then I'd pour myself a sherry. Relax.

I bent down to pick up some of the clutter from the floor, then rose again, perplexed. An unmistakeable whiff of Chanel no. 5 permeated the air.

My pulse began to race. Laura. She was here after all then.

I felt a quivering in my nostrils and began to sneeze. I have an allergy to that scent. I grabbed a tissue from the box.

Laura knew about my allergy. This was her way of winding me up. It set off flames of fury inside me, making me forget my fear and yell out, "What's up, Laura Nash? Still brooding about me and Mike? Even though he dumped me, and married you?"

My voice grew shrill, defiant. "I know it's you, by the way. I can smell your trademark."

She'd always been an extravagant bitch! Chucking Mike's money around on Gucci handbags and designer clothes! Why had she never got herself a job and paid for her luxuries with her own money, as I had? I work for my living. Have a book-keeping job in the City.

Heaven knows, though, how long I'll keep it. I'm making mistakes lately. Can't seem to focus. It's stress, the stress of losing Mike, and this other business … the Laura business. The investigation goes on; the questioning of suspects. She wasn't short of enemies.

I pushed such thoughts from my mind, yanked up an overturned pot of geraniums and slapped it back on the window-sill. Plants I could cope with. Mike's vase, no.

I went to the dresser, caressed the mutilated china body, dismembered mouth. The vase had been Mike's last gift. But then she knew that, didn't she? Little cow!

She'd got at the photograph too. The one of Mike and me on holiday in Venice. Crushed it into the carpet. Those tarty shoes with the spike heels had done it, I'll bet.

"You're so predictable, darling," I called out, affecting a bored smile. "So unoriginal. I know it's you. And I'm not afraid."

There came a noise like a peel of laughter, then a tinkling sound like silver bracelets dancing on a woman's arm. *Her* arm.

I stood rigid, heart pounding again. Where the hell was it coming from? My eyes darted round the room. I used not to believe in ghosts. But now… Was I perhaps hallucinating?

Silence followed, then paper rustling behind me.

I wheeled, and caught sight of the calendar above the dresser. Surely the date was wrong? Yes, someone had changed it. *She* had changed it. She'd brought September screaming back, with the 15th ringed in scarlet, and after it, two letters, blunt like hammer-blows: *L.N.* My mouth went dry. This was a new game.

"For Christ's sake, leave me alone!"

Limbs trembling, I staggered to the sofa and sat down, pressing my hands against my temples.

The phone rang. I grabbed it. "Yes?" I shouted into the receiver.

Heavy breathing. Then a voice, disguised. "You're still here then."

"Who is this?" I demanded.

"You'll soon find out. I'm very close." There came a shrill laugh.

"Sod off, you psycho!" I flung down the receiver. The voice had taunted me before. Someone was trying to drive me mad. What with weird phone calls *and* unearthly visitations!

I sat alert, waiting for a whisper, a mocking laugh, or some other sign of her presence. But there was only silence. Had she gone? No. I could still smell her scent.

Anger started up again. My head throbbed. Expletives tumbled out like vomit. "Bitch! Slut! What do you want with me? Go back to hell where you belong!"

No answer. Nothing except the slow drip-drip of a leaking tap. "Go away!" I screamed. "Go, with your bangles, your scent, your cow-breasts!" A sob rose to my throat. "Mike never cared about breasts till you came."

Not a sound.

Then the doorbell shrieking through the silence.

I made myself rise, walk calmly to the door.

Two men, waiting on the step, one well-built, grey, moustached, the other, younger, leaner.

My heart began to thump.

"Mr John Ridley?"

"That's me." I fingered the growth of stubble on my chin, wiped sweat off my forehead. "What d'you want?"

"Sorry to disturb you, Sir, but we're police officers, investigating the Laura Nash murder. May we come in?" He pushed a search-warrant under my nose. "You were a friend of Laura's husband, I understand, before he married? A very close friend?"

He coughed and turned away. The younger man smirked.

I nodded. The wind sighed through the trees. A dead leaf stroked my face. Slowly, I led them into the hall.

They halted at the living-room door, looking through.

"Your friend made quite a mess I see."

"My friend?"

"Mike Nash. He came here earlier today. Unwise perhaps. But he found what he wanted."

"No. Not Mike. He wouldn't trash my place." My heart went cold. Mike. Crushing our photograph, breaking the vase. Not Laura's ghost. Mike.

The younger one took out his notebook. "Now, Sir, could you tell us where you were on Friday, 15th September?"

I smiled, grimly, as I remembered the letters L.N scrawled on the calendar, the stuff under the wardrobe that Mike must have found.

"With Laura," I said, simply. "I shot the little hell-cat."

THE FOSTER CHILD

When I heard that Cousin Claudia was coming to stay, my stomach turned queasy and I almost threw up.

"It's only for Wednesday night, Adrian," my mother said, soothingly. "She's got an interview at Durham University. It'll be nice if she can spend the night here, instead of travelling from Hampshire and back in one day."

I shoved aside my half-finished omelette and groaned.

My mother sighed. "I can't think what you've got against her. She's become a really nice girl. And it's obvious she likes you. Remember those DVDs she brought you the last time she came?"

Honestly, my mother's so naïve! I could tell her a thing or two about Claudia. For one thing, she wasn't a `nice girl' by any standards. For another, she *didn't* like me. Any more than I liked her. Take those gifts she gave me. Tokens of friendship? Not by a long shot. They were *thrust* on me, to keep me quiet. The truth is, Claudia has a secret, and she knows I'm wise to it. This scares her like hell. Suppose, one day, I shout it out to the world, so *everyone* knows? She wouldn't want that. Hence the gifts.

She needn't worry. I won't tell. What's the point? It can't change anything. I just want her out of my life. Totally. We've kept out of each other's way for the last four years. Why spoil things? Does she think I've forgotten her secret?

If so, she's kidding herself. I'll never forget.

It's embedded in my mind. Every detail of those awful weeks spent with her family in Hampshire when we were both nine years old.

I'm eighteen now. But I remember it all as clearly as yesterday: the great, rambling house on the outskirts of the town; Aunt Amy and Uncle Gerald pottering in that enormous garden, with all its nooks and crannies; Claudia, playing with her brute of a dog, Zac; and Angie, the foster-child.

They got Angie to keep Claudia company, though I found out later this wasn't the main reason. Aunt Amy desperately wanted another child, but she'd had a hysterectomy and it wasn't possible. So they took on Angie.

And everyone adored her. You couldn't help it. To start with, she had the face of an angel, bordered by masses of gold curls. And she had this lovely nature. Though not yet eight, she knew just how to please, with her hugs and smiles and willingness to make the best of things. Now that I'm older and know a bit more about life, I'm amazed how a girl from a care home could have turned out so well.

Neighbours were dazzled. "Isn't she beautiful?" they'd coo. "Isn't she an absolute darling?" Then, as an afterthought, they'd turn to Claudia. "Aren't you lucky, dear, to have such a lovely new sister?" to which Claudia would reply, "She's not my sister."

Even I, young as I was, had a crush on Angie. I followed her everywhere, agreeing to play silly, girlie games that I usually despised. On one occasion, I even persuaded Aunt Amy to let me go shopping with them to buy Angie a new dress.

Aunt Amy was forever buying her stuff. I think it was partly because Angie was so overjoyed at receiving the smallest thing, and so pathetically grateful. She'd hug and kiss her foster-mother and say. "I do love you, Aunt Amy. More than anything in the world."

At this, Claudia would roll her eyes or make sick noises in her throat. Then she'd run off to find Zac, her beloved dog, and you wouldn't see her till tea-time.

There were times when I felt sorry for Claudia. It couldn't have been much fun having a foster-sister who excited so much attention, you were forever having to take a back seat, even with your parents.

At first, I thought she was too thick-skinned to notice, or that she didn't care. But I couldn't have been more wrong.

I realised this one tea-time when the subject of dolls arose.

"You never play with them, Claudia, not since you got Zac," her mother said, cutting a plum-cake into slices. "You can easily spare one to give to Angie."

She smiled pleadingly at her daughter who sat, poker-faced at the table, studying the pattern on the table-cloth. "You do still like Angie, don't you?" Her mother looked anxious a moment. "You assured Mrs Bloom from the agency that you got on well together."

"So I did," Claudia agreed, sulkily.

Aunt Amy seemed not to notice that Claudia spoke in the past tense.

"Good. I'd be disappointed if you two fell out." She paused. "So why not offer her Emily-Jane? It would be such a kind gesture ..." She stopped. Angie, arriving for tea, was standing at the dining-room door, listening.

"It's okay, Aunt Amy," she piped up in her fluty little voice. "I don't want the doll, if it's going to make Claudia sad."

Claudia glared at her. "You're welcome to it," she snapped. "I'm too big for dolls anyway."

Her mother smiled. "Good girl. I knew you'd be generous. It's nice to see you like each other enough to share things."

I snorted inwardly. What was wrong with Aunt Amy? Was she blind or what? Maybe at first, Claudia did like Angie, but not any more, to judge from her manner. Was my aunt so mad keen to foster a child that she deliberately ignored all signs of trouble?

The following day, as I was going upstairs, I heard muffled sobs. They seemed to come from Angie's bedroom. Now normally, when a girl cries, I beat it to the nearest exit. But with Angie, I became this knight in shining armour, ready to fight for her rights. So I knocked at the door. The sobs died away to a quiet snuffle. I went in.

She was sitting on the bed, her hands covering her eyes, shoulders shaking. Below her, lying on its front, was a doll with black plaits and a frilly dress.

I sat beside her.

She threw her arms around me and began to sob against my shoulder. "It's Em-Emily J-Jane," she choked out. "Look!" She turned and pointed to the doll.

I picked it up and gasped. The dress was torn to pieces down the front, and there were holes where her eyes should have been. Worse, her neck had been bitten through and left a mangled mess.

I flung it down. "Gross! Who on earth ...?"

Her face puckered up. "Zac. Claudia made him do it. She doesn't like me any more."

I put on a fierce look and jumped up. "Just you wait till I see Claudia. I've a good mind to tell Aunt Amy about this. She'll make her give you another doll."

"No, Adrian." Angie stopped crying. A look of fear crossed her face. "She said that if I tell, she'll do something bad to me. And she means it."

Later that day, Aunt Amy saw the damage for herself when she went up to change the beds. She tackled us about it during dinner.

"It was perfectly okay when I gave it to her," Claudia fibbed, shrugging her shoulders. There was not a sign of guilt on her face. "Angie's probably fed-up with it already."

I almost choked on my omelette. "You're a big liar!" I burst out, feeling myself go red. "*You're* the one who did it."

Uncle Gerald gave me a look. "That's enough, Adrian. Let Angie speak for herself."

Angie looked fearfully around her. Her eyes rested on Claudia. Claudia met her stare, a tiny smile hovering round her mouth. She was daring her to tell the truth.

Angie said nothing, but her face crumpled and she fled from the room.

Aunt Amy, lines of anxiety on her face, followed her. "Angie darling, it's all right. It's only a doll."

Uncle Gerald sighed as he finished up his coffee. "She's hiding a lot of anger, that child," he muttered.

"Not a good sign." He shook his head, got up and went out.

All the while, Claudia sat there, the smug smile on her face growing broader.

"Filthy liar!" I exploded, pushing at her chair as I went by.

I hardly spoke to her after that. But I kept my beady eyes on her just the same, especially when she was anywhere near Angie. I could guess what she was up to. She was hell-bent on poisoning her parents' minds so they'd send her back to the care home.

I waited for the next move.

It soon came. Angie's eighth birthday was due. And Aunt Amy promised to give her a great party with games outside, if it was fine, and a conjurer to entertain them.

"*I* never had a conjurer," Claudia said, as we sat in the garden. She picked up a stray foxglove and tore it into strips.

Her mother, doing some weeding nearby, frowned. "You got a clown," she reminded her. "Don't begrudge Angie a conjurer, Claudia. This will be her first party. Try to be happy for her."

That afternoon Aunt Amy took the girls into town to choose party frocks. Afterwards, they paraded in them in front of me and Mrs Frost, the daily help. Claudia's was yellow with a matching bow fastened at the neck. The colour went well with her dark hair.

"You like my dress, Mrs Frost?" she demanded, flashing her a smile.

"Very nice, dear," Mrs Frost said. But her eyes were on Angie in her white tulle dress with the blue sash. She gazed at her, enraptured. "Just look at little Angie! Isn't she a picture?"

I saw Claudia's smile fragment and disappear. She flung Mrs Frost a look of hate and stalked out. Once again she had been pushed into the shade.

On the night before the party we saw the signs of Claudia's revenge. Aunt Amy, busy preparing for the following day, came running down the stairs, face flushed, Angie's dress draped over her arm. "Angie, just look at your dress! Why, child, why?"

She held up the dress for us to see. I gave a whistle of dismay. There were streaks of red crayon down the front. And part of the tulle skirt was torn away from the bodice.

"How shocking!" Claudia gasped.

Aunt Amy turned to her sharply. "*You* don't know anything about this, do you, Claudia?"

"*Me?*" Her eyes widened. "You surely don't think I did it, Mummy?"

Her mother turned to Angie whose face was a picture of bewilderment. "It wasn't me, Aunt Amy. I wouldn't spoil my party-dress."

Aunt Amy looked ready to cry. "Well, *someone* did." She sank down on the sofa.

But she dropped the subject. I figured she'd sooner forget the whole thing than discover the culprit was Claudia. Conflict between the girls would have spoilt everything.

She sighed and said at last, "You'll have to wear your spotted dress tomorrow, Angie. With that sash, it should look almost as nice as your party-dress."

It didn't. Not half as nice. But when her birthday came, Angie soon cheered up and forgot about it.

The party started well. It was a beautiful August day and excited children skipped around the garden, eager to enjoy themselves. Some of the parents had come along to help.

Claudia insisted that Zac join the party. He ran around barking, gobbling up sausages or anything else that children dropped for him. It was mind-boggling to see what Claudia could do with that dog. He obviously doted on her. She showed us how he obeyed her commands to sit, catch, shake hands …

In the middle of this demonstration, Aunt Amy called for quiet. She led Angie onto the patio and clasped her hand. "Gather round, everyone, I've something to tell you."

Claudia, annoyed at the interruption, stayed where she was with Zac.

"Claudia!" Her mother, still clasping Angie's hand, stepped down from the patio and hurried towards her. "Didn't you hear me?"

Claudia scowled. "I was showing them something important. Now you've spoilt it."

"What I have to say, Claudia, is more important than a dog's tricks. Now just leave Zac, and try listening for a change. *Angie* listens. Why can't you?"

She strode off, Angie skipping at her side.

I saw Claudia's face redden, her eyes flash. Not good signs.

"Come on, Claudia," I coaxed. "You can play with Zac later."

"Shut up! And I wasn't `playing'." She glared at me, and if looks could kill, I'd have dropped dead there and then.

We joined the others, Claudia tight-lipped, her face twisted into a frown.

A moment later, her mood worsened.

Aunt Amy, on the patio with Angie, clapped her hands for silence. "Before we start the games, I've some wonderful news," she began. "We're going to adopt Angie and make her our own child. Claudia will have a true sister at last."

I suppose, for Claudia, this was the straw that broke the camel's back. I saw her eyebrows shoot up, then her fists clench as she muttered, "Not if I can help it."

After claps and congratulations, especially from parents, Aunt Amy said, "And now, before the birthday cake and the conjurer, we're going to play Hide-and-Seek. It's Angie's choice, so she'll be the seeker. Off you go! There are lots of hiding- places in this garden."

Claudia gave a snort of contempt. Her mood was making me nervous. I was afraid she'd ruin Angie's party. And Angie was so happy. To my relief, Claudia merely jumped up and called to Zac, "Come on boy, let's look for a place where Angie can't find us." They raced off.

I ran off too, choosing a hiding-place in the tool shed.

It took Angie fifteen minutes to find me. She laughed and grabbed my sleeve. "Got you! I've got everyone now, except Claudia. I'll never find *her*. She's so clever at hiding."

"Try the `Foxes' Den'," I suggested. "You know that's her special hidey-hole."

She ran off again, laughing. I joined the others.

We kicked a ball around while we waited. Some of the girls played 'Touch'.

Soon, squeals of pleasure rang out, as Mrs Frost arrived on the patio with the birthday cake. Someone clapped her hands and shouted, "Wow! Great!"

I turned round. It was Claudia. When did she get back? I wondered. And where was Angie? She'd been ages.

A general cry went up. "Where's Angie?"

"Still looking for me, I expect," Claudia said. "I got fed-up of waiting."

I felt a sudden chill. Perhaps she'd had an accident. "I'll go and find her," I said.

I raced to the far end of the garden and through a narrow archway which led to a patch of tangled weeds and a compost heap. Not far from the compost heap, amongst the trees behind, was the 'Foxes Den'. It was like a cave, made out of weeds and bits of branches.

"Angie!" I called "Angie!"

My heart was beating like mad. Not only from running, but from a strange feeling of dread.

As I got to the entrance of the den, a piece of yellow fabric on the ground caught my eye. The bow off Claudia's dress. I picked it up and put it in my pocket.

"Angie!" I called again.

Still no reply. Then I heard a low growl from inside the den.

A moment later, Zac appeared, his wolf-like body framed in the entrance. A dull, hammering fear started up inside me. His fur looked damp, and something trickled down the side of his jaw. He growled louder, his eyes menacing.

I picked up a fallen twig nearby. "Go on, boy, fetch!" I yelled, and threw it as far as I could into the distance.

He leapt out after it.

I stepped into the den. It was then that I saw the blood. Spattered everywhere, staining leaves and branches. And in the middle of it all, a child, lying horribly still, one leg twisted under the other. Angie. Her dress was ripped to pieces, her throat torn.

I waited for my heart to stop thudding, for my hands to stop shaking. Then I turned and fled, out of the den, through the archway, up the garden, yelling and screaming like a demented pig.

When the others saw me, the party fun stopped. I can see them all now, staring at me, open-mouthed, still, silent, Aunt Amy poised, statue-like over the birthday cake. Then, the whole garden and everything in it seemed to spin. That was when I fainted.

It was the end of the birthday party. The end of Angie.

Claudia had a story all prepared. "I hid in the hollow-tree," she explained, sham tears streaking her face. "There wasn't room for Zac, so he ran off. Angie must have teased him and made him angry."

I knew she was lying. "You were in the Fox's Den with Zac," I told her later. "You got him to attack Angie."

She opened her mouth to deny it, but I held up the yellow bow from her party-dress. "I found it outside the den," I said. "Poor Zac! He'll have to be put down. But it was *you* who made him do it. Murderer! Now you'll lose him. And it serves you right."

A defiant look crossed her face. "Okay, so I'll lose my dog," she snapped, "but I've got my parents back."

Of course, the bow wasn't real evidence. I could have found it anywhere in the garden. But Claudia wasn't taking any chances. "Don't tell on me, Adrian," she pleaded.

I should have told, but I didn't, for Aunt Amy's sake. More bad news would have sent her over the edge.

By way of appreciation, Claudia stuck one of her favourite video-games in my suitcase. When I got home, I flung it in the dustbin.

I wonder what she'll bring me when she comes up on Wednesday?

CELEBRITY

"God Almighty!" Alice Gunter lowered her copy of the Daily Mail, eyes like saucers, mouth agape. "He's done it again! That's the fourth."

"Who you on about, Ma? Done what?" Her son, Jamie, reluctantly closed volume two of *How to Make a Name for Yourself*, and glanced across at his mother with distaste. Curled up on the sofa, she bulged out of her fake-silk dressing-gown, looking, he thought, like some bloated arthropod about to burst from its cocoon. A pile of *Hullo* and *Okay* magazines lay beside her on the coffee-table next to an ash-tray full of cigarette butts. Jamie wrinkled his nose. What a sight! If only her so-called 'clients' could see her now!

She waved the paper at him. "Read it. It's that weirdo again who's been knocking off celebrities. It's Jenny Frost this time, that little presenter on Channel four, the one who went missing. I've worked for her once or twice. Lovely girl." Her voice sank to a whisper. "It's terrible the state she was in when they found her. Face slashed. Head bashed in. Obscene things scribbled over her body!"

"Yeh, I already read it. Terrible." Jamie turned back to his book.

She pursed her lips. "They'll never catch him. Too clever. Leaves no finger-prints, DNA. Nothing."

Jamie smiled. "I bet *I* could catch him, if I were a detective."

"*You?*" His mother's face twisted into a look of scorn. "The only thing *you* could catch is a cold." She picked up her cigarette lighter, then glanced around the room, eyes flickering with annoyance. "Where the hell are my fags?"

"On the sideboard, Ma, where you left them."

"Well?" She glared at him.

With a sigh, Jamie pulled his wiry body out of the armchair, crossed to the sideboard and picked up the packet of Dunhill lying on the top.

She snatched it from him and gave him a sharp look. "You been to the job-centre this morning yet?"

"Give us a chance, Ma. It's only half past nine."

"Well, don't forget." She lit a cigarette and took a long drag. "I can't think why you didn't stay at that last job. It was you to a tee."

Jamie frowned. "What? Stacking shelves at Tesco's?"

"So? Better than sitting on your arse all day, doing nothing."

Waves of indignation leapt up inside him. "I went to university, don't forget …"

"Oh, yes. Media Studies. I remember." She gave a sniff of contempt. "A lot of good it did you too, dropping out after six months. And there was I thinking you were about to get somewhere."

"I got some acting jobs afterwards."

She rolled her eyes. "As an extra. Call that acting?"

"I got a couple of walk-ons as well. What about that policeman I did in *East Enders*? Or that ambulance driver in *Casualty*?" His voice rose. "How do you know I wouldn't do better than those soap stars you rattle on about, if I only had a chance? It's all luck. You got to be in the right place at the right time."

"You'll never be in the right place." His mother pushed back a strand of bleached hair from her face and heaved a sigh. "You've been a cab-driver, a salesmen, a pharmacist's assistant ... shall I go on? And you're not thirty yet. You're a complete loser."

Jamie had an urge to slap her in the mouth with one of her *Hullo* magazines, but as usual, he restrained himself. "I'll make you proud of me yet, Ma," he murmured. "Perhaps one day *I'll* become a celebrity."

She gave a hoot of laughter. "That'll be the day." She stubbed out her cigarette, leaned back on the sofa and eyed him, coldly. "You're pathetic, you know that? Celebrity! Don't make me laugh. I know about celebrities. I write their letters, fill in their engagement books ..." She gave a smirk. "I know all their secrets too."

Jamie grinned. She was right about that. She was forever telling him who was doing what where in the celebrity world. But making out she was some high-powered personal assistant! Did she think he was born yesterday? She was a *cleaner*, damn it. He'd spied on her a few times and caught her at it, fetching, carrying ... It drove him mad. His mother! Skivvy to those spoilt, overpaid, strutting-about show-offs.

He viewed her through narrowed eyes as she lit another cigarette. "It's you who's pathetic, not me," he muttered under his breath. "And don't tell me they trust you with their secrets. What you do is snoop through their engagement books, listen in to their phone calls. That's how you know what's happening."

He watched his mother drop specks of ash over her dressing-gown and flick them off. "You shouldn't smoke so much, Ma. You'll get lung-cancer."

"Oh, shut your face. It's the only comfort I've got."

He rose and walked over to the sofa, the smell of cigarette ash irritating his nostrils. "Can I shift some of these magazines? They're taking up an awful lot of space on the coffee-table."

His mother clapped a protective hand over the pile. "You leave them alone, you little rat-bag. I know you. You'll sneak them into your room to read, and that's the last I'll see of them. Get me a coffee. Do something useful for a change."

Nodding meekly, Jamie made his way to the kitchen, shutting the door on his mother's voice.

Alone at last, he let the torrent of trapped rage, hot as larva, boil to the surface. Making his hands into fists, he crashed them down on the worktop, simultaneously letting out growls of *Bitch! Bitch! Bitch*! Then, face distorted with fury, he advanced upon the waste-bin and kicked it from one end of the kitchen to the other.

He paused to get his breath back. "Cool it, man," he murmured. He went to the fridge, took out a carton of milk and poured a few drops into the coffee cup. As he did so, he dreamed of mixing it with a strong dose of barbiturates that would send his mother into a deep sleep. It would be easy then to choke the life out of her. He'd do it with the belt of that fake-silk dressing-gown.

He sniggered. It was a happy thought, but hardly practical. If his mother were dead, how could he study her reaction, see the amazement, the disbelief on her face when he became a celebrity? Better to hang on until she heard the news. It would be worth the wait.

He grew calmer as he waited for the kettle to boil. A smile broke out on his face. They'd probably write books about him, once they found out how special he was. Maybe he'd have a go at writing his autobiography. Everyone would want to buy it, because everyone would want to know more about the amazing James Gunter. He chuckled. His mother wouldn't come out too well.

The kettle came to the boil. From behind the kitchen door, he heard the muffled call of his mother, "What the devil you doing in there, Jamie? Hurry up. My tongue's hanging out for that damned coffee."

"Coming, Ma."

He made a face and stuck up two fingers at the door. It was enough to make you puke, he thought, the way his mother ran around after those celebrities. And some of them had no talent to speak of. He picked up the kettle. He'd make a better presenter any day than that stupid, smiley Jenny Frost that they all fussed about. That show needed a *man*, someone with presence.

As for that earlier gonner, Maggie Ash, talk about ham. She'd had the cheek to treat him like cat's sick too, that time he'd done a walk-on in one of her films. His jaw tightened. He'd heard all about her going into a restaurant in Soho and demanding the best table. `Sorry, Madam, but it's not available,' the waiter told her. She'd stuck out her chest and answered, "But don't you know who I am?" Arrogant bitch!

"Hurry up," came his mother's voice again.

Jamie poured water into his mother's coffee-cup, stuck two custard-creams into the saucer beside it and carried them into the sitting-room.

"About time too."

He picked up the current issue of *Hullo* magazine and flicked through the pages. He paused at page twelve and whistled as he read a piece at the bottom. Well, well, so Polly James, that soap star his mother raved about, was holding a grand party tonight at Montague Mansions. Interesting.

He dropped the magazine on top of the rest of the pile.

He got up.

"Where you going?"

"To the Job Centre."

Better show willing. He pushed back a stray wisp of fair hair and drifted out. At the stairway he paused. First, he'd make sure everything was ready for tonight.

He hurried to his bedroom and opened the bottom drawer of the chest, pulled aside the bath towel which lay at the top and peered underneath. Yes, everything in order. Hammer, knife, rope, chloroform, latex gloves, false moustache. He'd add a bar of soap this time too. And stick it in her stupid soap-star mouth, as a final twist.

He smiled. He knew Montague mansions well, and how to gatecrash Polly's party and get her to himself. He was nothing, if not resourceful.

Only, after this little job, he'd give himself up. Four times he'd outwitted those fools of detectives. But he had to get caught if he wanted to be famous and remembered for all time. He couldn't wait for ever for them to catch him.

And if I'm hated, he thought as he shut the drawer, so what? Better to be hated than ignored.

In this life, he reflected, you're either a celebrity or a nobody. He'd been a nobody for long enough. It was time to make a name for himself.

A PERFECT GENTLEMAN

The wrought-iron bench, behind the willow, was rusting in places and, unlike the others that overlooked the lake, it had a slat missing and another one loose. But to Margaret Bunn it was the finest bench in Regents Park, for it was the one she shared with Mr Videl, the courtly gentleman with the gold-topped stick, who often sat there.

Margaret couldn't call him a *friend* exactly. Their meetings were too casual. Yet, a mere glimpse of his silver hair, or whiff of his spice-scented skin sent her mind reeling, and the blood rushing through her veins in an almost-forgotten surge of excitement. She longed to be cocooned in his arms, spirited away to some fantasy-world where youth and love were eternal.

In steadier moments she'd mock her dreams. "Give over. You're pushing sixty, not sixteen."

Nevertheless, she felt *drawn* to him, like a moth to a lighted candle. And, following their first chance meeting in Regents Park, Margaret wandered there again and again, eager to find Mr Videl, sitting in his usual spot, on the bench behind the willow, overlooking the lake.

Directly she caught sight of his silver hair or his gold-topped stick, her eyes would light up and she'd murmur, "Perhaps today he'll want my number, today he'll ask me out."

But he never did.

She'd scold herself then. "Get real. You might be single again and Mr Videl might be unattached, but he's distinguished enough to attract a much younger woman, someone clear eyed and unwrinkled." Margaret would sigh at that thought and yearn to recapture her youth when men flocked around and made her feel a Queen.

But she never gave up her chance-meetings. And today was sunny and warm, perfect for meeting her dream-man in nearby Regents Park.

She pushed aside the half-finished crossword she'd been tackling. She'd lost focus. Anyway, she couldn't make head or tail of eight across. Could it be an anagram?

The solution would have to wait. Regents Park was calling her.

She got up, dressed carefully, and set off, crossing her fingers that Mr Videl would be there.

As she entered the gates and strolled towards the lake, her heart began to flutter and her hands to tremble as she spied him, straw-hatted and relaxed on the bench overlooking the water.

Seeing her approach, he smiled, rose and doffed his hat in greeting.

And, as ever, Margaret was enchanted.

"Ah, Ms Bunn. What a pleasure to have so attractive a lady sit beside me!"

She blushed. "Attractive, Mr Videl? At my age? Hardly."

"I disagree." He gave her a close look. "I'm sure you were a real head-turner at one time."

"Perhaps … when I was young. But now …" She heaved a sigh.

His look became more penetrating. She lowered her eyes and quaked a little.

"Take heart, Ms Bunn," he said at last. "There are ways of cheating time."

"Excuse me?" She looked up, startled.

He smiled and said, softly, "I'm a chemist, as you know, retired, but still dabbling. I've perfected a face-cream …"

"A face-cream?" She was intrigued, if sceptical. She had tried umpteen creams which promised miracles. None of them worked.

He drew a jar from his pocket. "As it happens I'm carrying a sample. Here, take it."

She trembled as their hands touched. His fingers were cool and competent, as thrill-inducing to Margaret as an aphrodisiac. She studied the jar. It was labelled: `Videlbond'.

"Apply each morning," he said, "and let me know how you get on. Don't forget."

"Where can I contact you?" Hope stirred. Perhaps now he'd give her his number or, at least his email address. She felt too shy, too fearful of rejection, to offer hers.

But all he said was, "Here. The usual place."

Unscrewing the lid, she sniffed at the oat-coloured cream. There was a hint of earth about the smell, of rushing water, underground caverns … She sniffed again, dreaming a while of beauty and of love …

She asked, "How much do I owe you, Mr Videl?"

There was no reply.

She turned towards him.

And a shadow fell over her heart and hung there. He had gone. She looked across the park and saw him walking towards the gates, his gold-topped stick tapping along beside him.

She rose. Ah well, they'd meet again. He'd want to know how she got on with his cream.

The following morning, Margaret dabbed it over her face, inspecting herself in the bathroom-mirror. No change. Really, what did she expect?

But, later that day, things started to happen. She felt a tightening and tingling, deep in her skin, as if her face were going through a renaissance. She rushed to the mirror again.

- And gave a gasp of wonder.

The cream had worked. Scarcely a line or wrinkle in sight, her cheeks plumped out, her lips full. It was a metamorphosis.

A whirlwind week followed. She invited friends round to show off her youthful looks. Her daughter came. "Heavens, Mum, that's the best face-lift I've ever seen!" she breathed. "You look thirty-five."

She went several times to Regents Park to find Mr Videl, partly to get hold of more cream, partly to find out if now, seeing her recovered beauty, he'd finally want to date her.

But each time, that special bench overlooking the lake was empty.

She wasn't too disheartened. These days younger, handsomer men asked her out: Tom from the Unitarian church; Ralph, the young lawyer she'd met at the Bridge Club. They'd hardly noticed her before. Their attention lifted her spirits. She no longer felt invisible, of no account, but walked with a bold stride, feeling that the whole world smiled at her.

But the cream was coming to an end. In a couple of months there was nothing left.

Margaret hurried to Regents Park, but still no Mr Videl.

She grew anxious.

A frantic searching on the internet brought no success. There was no website, no information at all for a pharmacist named Alfred Mephisto Videl.

Very soon, her worst fears were realised: the reversal of her metamorphosis. At first, Margaret felt a loosening under her skin, as if muscle and tissue were wasting away. Then, with growing dread, she saw in her mirror the steady hollowing of her cheeks and eye-sockets, the thinning of her lips, the return of her wrinkles.

She stopped phoning her friends, dropped her lovers.

It might seem shallow, she thought, but looks do matter. And what else do I have to offer? Nothing.

At last, on a hurried visit to Regents Park, she saw him, legs crossed, hat rakishly askew, on his favourite bench.

She rushed forward and sank beside him, breathless. "The cream, Mr Videl, it's finished."

A smile lurked at the corners of his mouth. "Relax, Ms Bunn, relax! So, you've lost your youthful looks?" He shook his head and chuckled. "Poor Ms Bunn!"

She tightened her lips. He was mocking her, revelling in her discomfort, probably thinking, `silly, pathetic old woman, wanting her youth and beauty back!' For the first time she felt a prickle of dislike for Mr Videl.

But she needed him. Now more than ever.

"I tried to see you before," she said, reproach in her voice, "but you were never here. And you've never given me a contact number."

"Oh, I never divulge my number, even to you, Ms Bunn." A smile, dark with secrets, hovered about his mouth.

"Then how do I reach you when I run out of cream?"

He patted her knee. "I'll be here, my dear, waiting for you. Not immediately perhaps, but … finally."

She gave an impatient sigh. "Your cream's a miracle, and I'm grateful. I hope to purchase several jars." When I finish one, she thought, I can start on another. Then I'll be safe.

He shook his head. "I'm afraid it's one jar at a time. The cream must be fresh, you see."

Her face clouded.

He took her hand and stroked it. Unlike the last time, his hand felt cracked and dry, his fingers bony. She flinched. With a shock, she realised that Mr Videl had begun to repel her.

Has he changed or have I? she asked herself.

But he was still important. He was the maker of her miracle-cream.

"Please give me what you've got then, Mr Videl."

Dark ripples of laughter rose from his throat. "I believe you'd do anything to get your beauty back, you minx."

"Perhaps. What is it you want?" Her feelings had changed but, to get hold of that cream, she'd have gone to his bed, had he insisted.

He drew a sheet of folded paper and a pen from his pocket and handed them to her. "Just your signature here, please, to confirm receipt of my beauty treatment."

"My signature!" Margaret echoed. A small price to pay, she thought, for a cream that's priceless.

She glanced at the sheet. The print was too tiny to read but vanity demanded she leave her glasses behind.

She could just make out the dotted line at the bottom. She signed her name there with a flourish.

He almost snatched the document from her, his eyes glittering like black beads.

Then he drew out the jar of cream. Seeing how eagerly she stretched out to grab it, he held it back teasingly, and clicked his tongue. "Dear, oh dear, how tempting is the sin of vanity!"

He finally gave it to her. She thrust it into her handbag and snapped it shut.

"You will go on supplying me?" she asked, her voice edged with panic.

"Until the supply dries up."

She frowned. "But why should it dry up? You're a chemist. You can surely make more?"

His lips twitched in amusement. "Beauty can't last for ever. Nor can my beauty cream."

"But what will I do when I can't get more?"

He bent over her, peering into her face, hands clasped over the gold knob of his stick, looking, for all the world, Margaret thought, like a hungry eagle. She shrank away.

"You'll become very old," he replied, "and when the creaks and groans of old age hit, you'll not care about looks any more. There's nothing like pain for focussing the mind." He let out a hoarse chuckle which sounded to Margaret like dirty water gurgling into a sewer. Next moment, he grasped her hand, savagely this time, squeezing it until she cried out.

"And when all ends," he continued, his voice sinking to a whisper, "you'll come to me, you understand?"

"No!" She twisted out of his grasp.

She didn't want to go to him. Not anymore. How had she ever found him attractive? He was scarcely human. Fear gripped her, and she gasped, "Who are you?"

His laughter crackled over the water.

At last he spoke. "The answer is in my name." He said it with a smile that chilled her.

Then he rose from the wrought-iron bench with its spreading patch of rust and delivered a sharp tap with his stick to the loosened slat behind him. It dropped with a clang to the ground. Finally, he turned and touched his hat. "Till we meet again, Ms Bunn."

As he strode off, the sky darkened. A clap of thunder shattered the air. Passers-by looked up, startled, and hastened to the park-gates.

Drops of rain, like tears, fell upon Margaret's head. She scarcely felt them, as she pondered his words: "The answer is in my name."

"Videl" she murmured. She thought of her unfinished crossword at home. Then the truth hit her like a stone. His name was an anagram.

Still as a corpse, she sat slumped on the run-down, rusting bench, heedless of its second missing slat. She stared across the lake. And as she stared, it seemed to empty itself of water, leaving a dark, gaping hole. She shut her eyes. Her throat tightened. The bitter question jangled like a bell, through her brain. What price beauty now? Now that she'd signed her soul to the devil, and saw how it would all end?

OBSESSED

"I came to you as a last resort." Voice trembling, she hovers at my living-room door.

I wait, silent.

We've not met before, not face-to-face, but I know who she is. I've seen her on stage, and caught glimpses of her, out with Richard. She's Emma Flynn, and, like him, she's in show-business. He's described her to me, in tones of hushed triumph, as if he's caught an angel in his net.

I let my eyes sweep over her. She's nothing like me. I'm tall, strong, with bold features and hair the colour of coal. And she? Oh, she's a doll, a cherry-lipped blonde with dainty gestures and sex-appeal oozing from every pore.

I can see she's pregnant. The bulge is beginning to show. And I know it's Richard's child she's carrying. He told me.

She takes a faltering step into the room, imploring me with her eyes. "I don't know what to do. I've been to the police, contacted his agent ..." Her hands flutter as if to scoop answers from the air. "He's just vanished."

She moves towards me, plucks at my sleeve. "Please, I'm desperate. Do you have any idea where Richard is? I know he came here." Her mouth tightens. "He had to. To make you stop."

She drops her hand and turns away. "I was with him sometimes when he checked his phone for messages. Those interminable calls from you! The emails, every damned day!" Her voice rises. "You just wouldn't let him go. You were obsessed."

I was. I know that now. So obsessed that just a sight of him would console me; the mere sound of his voice make my day. That's all there was towards the end: a disembodied voice, or a tangle of wild hair glimpsed as he turned a corner. I drank them in: sight and sound, clung to them, as if my very existence depended on these brief reminders of the love I'd lost.

"We adored each other," I say.

"He was *attracted* to you – at first," she counters, "but you were too all-over-him, too needy. It put him off." Her voice softens, becomes patronising. "You're not bad-looking. You could have easily found someone else. But you wouldn't leave him alone, would you? You even stalked him."

I wince. True again. I followed him, slunk about outside his flat. I couldn't cope with a single day without seeing him or hearing his voice.

Something cold shivers in my memory: the day he ended it all. "I've got a role in the new musical, *Bling*. It's going to be hectic the next few weeks – rehearsing and so on. I won't have time to see you, Ros. Sorry."

"But we can meet after rehearsals," I said, "Go over your script."

He shuffled his feet then, looked down at the floor. "No. It's best we stop seeing each other for a while. Give ourselves some space, eh? I'm not ready for anything long term."

That's when I gulped out my news. "I'm pregnant."

He straightened, horror flooding his face. "Pregnant? Weren't you on the pill?"

"I thought you loved me … and it didn't matter."

"Good God, woman, I'm an actor, as often resting as working. I can't support a child."

He took out his diary. "How far gone are you?" He began flicking through it for the dates we'd met. "Are you sure it's mine?"

Anger tightened my chest. "You know there's no one else."

He began to pace the room, jaw clenched. "You'll have to get rid of it."

"No!" It had been the fulfilment of a dream, bearing Richard's child. How could I destroy it?

I argued. I wept. But he had his way. Worn down by his begging and pleading, his persistent moans that I'd wreck his career, and that I'd never cope on my own, my determination crumbled and I agreed to get rid of the child. Weak of me perhaps, but I still adored him and I couldn't let him go away hating me and feeling I was a rope round his neck.

For months after the abortion, part of me seemed to die. I dragged myself, zombie-like through each day that passed, eating little, sleeping less, giving up on life.

Then, one evening, flicking through a newspaper, I caught sight of a piece about *Bling* with a picture of Richard and other actors from the show. As I gazed at it, a sudden wriggle of hope started up. Perhaps he'll see me again, I thought. I've kept away, given him space, got rid of the child. Perhaps now he's missing me, but too proud to get in touch.

I phoned him, a smile in my voice. "It's Rosalind, Richard. I saw your picture in the paper. The show's doing well, it seems. I'm glad for you."

He sounded happy, friendly. "Thank you, Ros. It's only a short run though, and comes to an end in a few months. If you haven't seen it, and you're free, I can get you tickets for Monday night. Tell you what, why don't I drop them in tomorrow on my way to the theatre?"

I caught my breath. I was going to see him again. Energy came bounding back. Already, I could feel his cheek brushing mine, smell the lemony tang of his after-shave.

On the day he was due to come, I dressed carefully, wearing my new drop-earrings shaped like hearts, and the black, slinky trousers that he liked so much. Shivers of excitement danced up and down my spine as I heard the doorbell ring and dashed out to greet him.

He glanced quickly at his watch. "I can't stay long, Ros, but, hey, it's nice to see you." He plonked himself on my sofa and peered at me, his eyes resting on my waistline. "You're okay now, I take it?"

I shook off a pang of bitterness. "Don't worry. I didn't change my mind about the abortion."

He did nothing to choke back his sigh of relief.

"And how's your love-life?" I made my tone casual, even yawned as I asked the question.

His whole face seemed to light up. "It's amazing. At last, I've found someone I really care about. Her name's Emma, and she's playing one of the leads in the show. She's a terrific actor." His eyes grew dreamy. "I'm hoping to persuade her to move in with me – even marry."

My heart sank. "Does she want to marry you?"

He sighed. "I'm not sure. She's a bit out of my league."

I smiled. There was hope for me yet then.

I knew his landline number and phoned him frequently during the weeks that followed, anxious to find out how his romance was going. At first, his response was friendly enough, but soon his manner cooled, and I sensed an edge of irritation in his tone.

Finally, he burst out, "You must stop ringing, Ros. It's too much. You and I are finished. If you're thinking I might leave Emma and come back to you, you're living in Cloud Cuckoo Land. It's not going to happen."

His words cut me like a knife.

He sighed then. "Sorry, Ros. But you must get on with your own life. So stop phoning, okay?"

That's when I changed tactics. Desperate for some sort of contact, however tenuous, I'd phone him from an old phone box that still worked, wait for him to speak, then listen in silence, till he swore and banged down the receiver. At the same time, I started following him and hanging about outside his flat.

I turn my mind to the present, to Emma. She's stepping towards the French windows now, looking out at the garden, hands pressed against her head. It's making me uneasy.

"He had to change his landline number," she whinges. "*And* his email address. He even thought of calling the police. But you know all that already." She swings round to face me. "Because he came to see you about it, didn't he? To try and make you stop."

I bite my lip. I remember it well. First, the curt phone call. "Are you in this evening? *Bling's* finished its run, so I'm free. And Emma's away, visiting her parents."

He made himself comfortable on my green, upholstered chair, facing the French windows. He drew his tongue over his lips. "Listen, Ros," he began, "Emma and I have talked this over. You need help - counselling or something. The way you're acting isn't normal. And Emma's getting nervous." He paused, smoothed back his tangle of hair. "She's pregnant, you know. She could lose the baby."

"It's yours?" I felt my stomach tighten. "Does that mean she's going to marry you?"

"She's coming round to the idea."

"She could always have an abortion," I snapped, "as I did."

"She won't. And I'm glad. I really want this baby."

So, he *wants* this baby. Anger tore at me. And hate. It built up like a furnace in my chest, choking out love, and spurring me into action. I jumped up, controlled the tremor in my voice, and put on a smile. "I'm so happy for you, Richard, and I'm sorry I made you cross. It won't happen again."

I moved towards him. "Let's forget the past, shall we, and celebrate the good news? I've got some champagne."

I reached into the cupboard where two bottles stood waiting for some special occasion. I drew one out and stepped behind him …

Emma is still hovering at the French windows, staring ahead. I feel a throbbing at my temples. "Don't look at the garden, please," I say. "It's a mess. Sit down, do."

She perches at the edge of the chair Richard used to sit in, hands clasped, frowning. "I couldn't care less about your garden. My only concern is finding Richard."

She stares across at me. "What's happened, Rosalind? He wouldn't just stop calling me. Not unless something was terribly wrong." She throws her up her arms. "If you know where he is, for God's sake tell me."

I shrug. "How do you know he hasn't dumped you? He's an actor, isn't he, as often *resting* as working? Maybe he's thought twice about burdening himself with a child."

She glares at me. "You're wrong. He's as keen on this baby as I am."

She pauses, picks up her handbag and clicks it open.

"I'm convinced you know something about this. He visited you two weeks ago. It's all here in his diary – date, time, everything. It's his last entry. And since that visit, he hasn't been seen."

She draws a black leather diary from her handbag and holds it out. "I found it at Richard's flat yesterday. That's why I came over. I shall take it to the police. They'll probably want to question you."

She shuts her handbag, jumps up and marches to the door.

"No, wait." I plunge after her. "Richard called that day, yes. We drank champagne. To celebrate your pregnancy. Then he left …" My voice trails off.

"I don't believe you." She looks at me through narrowed eyes, turns, and sweeps out.

I watch her go. Then, knees trembling, I stumble back to the French windows, to stare into the garden.

Unease knots my stomach. She'll go to the police, I know. And they'll come here, asking questions, sniffing about. And if they go into the garden...

My heart is pounding now. Again I see myself grasping that champagne bottle, standing behind Richard and smashing it down on his head. Again I see his body slumping forward, blood streaming over the carpet.

I push away the image and draw a deep, calming breath. I've dealt with the carpet. Now for the garden. I'll do some digging – even it all up before the police come, so they don't see that dark patch at the bottom. I can say I've been planting bulbs ready for the spring.

I unlock the back door, put on my garden boots and fetch a spade from the shed. While I dig, I struggle to get my mind in order, to plan a way out of this mess. But all I can think of are Richard's words, `I *want* this baby … I *want* this baby …'

They go over and over in my head, like the rhythmic thud of my spade turning over the soil.

HOCUS-POCUS

I stumble upon the class photograph while clearing out an old bookcase in the loft. My heart gives a jolt. We were eleven when that photo was taken. That makes it more than sixty years old. No wonder it's so faded.

I carry it downstairs to study in a better light.

And there we are: Class 4a, sitting in neat rows in the school hall. On the left stands Miss Harris, the headmistress. She's short and plump, wearing a cameo-brooch at her neck. On the right is Mr Cording, our teacher, a big man with a mop of greying hair and fleshy lips.

I chuckle. We look so old-fashioned, the girls in gym-slips and white ankle-socks, boys in short trousers. I'm in the second row, skinny plaits dangling over my chest, a smile plastered on my face.

My eyes wander from one child to another. I can recall the names of most of the kids here: Helen, Glenys, George … And, next to me, Shirley Fox, my best friend. Her face is round and freckly, framed by a mouse-coloured bob. And, as usual, she's staring into space.

My eyes turn from her to Mr Cording. In my imagination, I see him aiming a board-rubber at her again, and Shirley cringing, her small shoulders hunched forward, her chin meeting her chest.

The years roll back. Once again I see the rows of heavy desks with ink-wells set in each, smell the chalk and hear it squeaking against the blackboard, feel the heat of the classroom stove on my face. And I hear again that rasping voice of Mr Cording yelling out: "Wake up, Fox!"

It made my blood boil the way Mr Cording forever picked on Shirley. Over and over again he'd bawl out, "Half-wit!" or "Silly ass!" if she gave the wrong answer. Sometimes, he'd whack her on the hand with his ruler, or throw a piece of chalk at her head. Once, he dragged her to the front of the class, swung her round and round, and finally threw her into an empty desk. Today you could sue him for that. Years ago, you put up with it.

Not that Shirley was any angel. I'd sometimes see her, miles away, dreaming out of the window, or slyly reading a comic when she should have been doing her geography or maths. Still, she didn't deserve all Mr Cording's put-downs. She had plenty of talent and worked hard at stuff she enjoyed. She wrote great stories, could draw and model things in clay better than anyone, and when it came to reading aloud, she did it with *feeling*, not in a dull monotone like the rest of us.

What bugged old Cording, I think, was that Shirley made no effort in maths, his favourite subject. On top of that, she was plain and shabbily-dressed. I couldn't help noticing that attractive children like Vera Matthews or Ben Clark, never got pushed around, even though they weren't particularly clever or attentive.

Shirley took her medicine like a lamb but, underneath, I could tell, trouble was brewing. It came to the boil one day when she read out a piece of prose so dramatically that at the end some of us clapped. Not

Mr Cording. He put on a falsetto voice and mocked her. For Shirley this was the last straw. After school that day, she said to me quietly, "I'm going to kill Mr Cording."

There was something so chilling in the way she said it that I didn't attempt to laugh it off. Instead, I mumbled, "Don't be daft. You *can't*."

"Yes I can." She spoke through her teeth. "I'll kill him by witchcraft. My Aunt Jenny's got books about it, about how to give you fits, or make your blood freeze up till you wither and die …"

I rolled my eyes. Witchcraft! She lived in a world of make-believe. "So your auntie's a witch?"

"Sort of." She turned and clutched at my arm. "Will you help me, Joan? You *are* my best friend. Best friends always help each other."

I shook her off. "You must be joking. I don't even believe in witchcraft, so how can I help?"

A smile twitched the corners of her mouth. "You can start by helping me nick some of Mr Cording's things: his hankie, strands of hair, and stuff."

I gaped at her. "You're bonkers! What for?"

She heaved an impatient sigh. "To do the magic, of course."

I gave her a push. "No. It's stealing. We'll get caught"

She shook her head. "Not if we're careful. We can hunt through his desk for stuff playtime, when no one's about. And getting hair will be easy. Even *you* could do that. Have you seen how bits fall out onto his desk when he pushes it back?"

I heard the glee gathering in her voice. "Soon as I've got enough things, I'll make a wax effigy of him, and set them all around it."

"And then what?"

She narrowed her eyes. "Then I stick pins into it, and one right through its chest till it pierces the heart. Then it's goodbye, Mr Cording."

She waved a hand in the air, then turned to me, flushed with excitement. "Well, are you game?"

I hummed and hawed. Then I thought, why not? It's all fantasy. We're stuck with Mr Cording for the rest of the year, like it or not. A bit of hocus-pocus might liven things up. "Okay," I said.

It wasn't long before I got a chance to pick up some loose hair. I spotted a tuft on Mr Cording's shoulder while I was standing at his desk getting my work marked. I slyly plucked it off, and shoved it in my pocket.

But he must have felt my touch. He looked up sharply and growled, "What are you doing, girl?"

"Bit of f-fluff on your jacket, Sir." I stammered, heart thumping. "It's off now."

He frowned but said no more.

Another time we sneaked into the classroom when it was empty and found a photo of him and his wife inside his desk. Shirley pounced on it. "What spiffing luck!"

We had nothing against his wife, so we cut her out and threw that piece away.

Later in the week Shirley snipped a button off the jacket he'd left on his chair. I pinched his nail file. He never asked about them or about the photo. Perhaps he hadn't noticed they'd gone.

The last thing we nicked was his cigarette lighter. Most people smoked in those days, even teachers. You could see the nicotine on their fingers and smell tobacco on their breath.

I was against taking the lighter. It looked expensive and felt too much like real stealing.

Mr Cording soon missed it. "Has anyone seen my lighter?" he demanded. Kids glanced at each other, shrugging or shaking their heads. I didn't know where to put myself.

"I'm sure it was on my desk." He stood up, frowning, and peered round the class, his eyes finally resting on me. I quaked and stared down at the floor.

To my relief, he turned away. "All right, get on with your work. It's probably in the staffroom."

I gave Shirley a dirty look. "That's the last time I'm helping," I muttered.

I needn't have worried. "We've got enough stuff now," she said, rubbing her hands. "I've already finished the effigy. It's a smashing likeness. That photo was a great help." She lowered her voice. "I'm going to do the magic tonight. Coming?"

Details of the night's ritual are blurred in my mind now. But I fancy I can still smell that wax image and still feel Shirley's hard little hands gripping mine as she chanted her gobbledygook. I can see the fierce set of her mouth, too, and the way her eyes glittered as she stuck each pin into Mr Cording's effigy.

It's only a game, I told myself. We both know it won't work. At the same time I could feel my insides starting to wriggle about in panic.

When we filed into the classroom the following morning, my panic got worse.

Mr Cording wasn't there. Kids chattered, fooled around, or read comics while they waited. Shirley nudged me, a funny little half-smile on her face.

"He's just late," I told her in an off-hand tone. But, inside, my stomach was churning, and I kept looking at the door, willing Mr Cording to appear.

Soon, a strong whiff of talcum powder and eau-de-cologne heralded the arrival of Miss Harris into the classroom. There was an instant hush as her eyes swept sternly over the class. "*I* shall be teaching you today," she began. She paused. A solemn note darkened her voice. "Mr Cording won't be here, I'm sorry to say. He was rushed into hospital late last night."

Gasps filled the classroom. I felt I was going to be sick. She went on, "It's come as a great shock and, this afternoon, we're each going to make a *Get Well* card to send him."

I could feel Shirley nudging my elbow again. She affected a look of concern, but the glint in her eyes worried me.

The following day Miss Harris brought us even worse news:

Her voice trembled slightly as she said, "I am sorry to have to tell you … but Mr Cording passed away late last night… I know you are all…"

Her last words were drowned by shocked cries from the class. A sob broke out from one of the girls.

I sat petrified, while the horror of what we'd done seeped into my brain. The magic had worked. We had killed Mr Cording.

I stole a glance at Shirley. Her face was flushed. She didn't mean to *kill* him, I thought. She must be as shocked as I am.

But I was wrong. The flush on her face was the flush of triumph. "See," she murmured, "I told you my magic would work, didn't I? People had better watch out in future, and not treat me like dirt."

We drifted away after that. My old friend had begun to scare me.

Near the end of the term I found I'd passed for the grammar school. Shirley had failed. She'd be going to the Secondary Modern. She could have passed, easily. But she refused to knuckle down for Mr Cording. She blamed *him* for that, and said she was glad he was dead.

I come out of my reverie, the photo still in my hand. Shirley and I lost touch years ago. Her family moved away late that summer. I often wonder how she is and if she ever tried any more magic.

I never told her the truth about Mr Cording. She'd already gone by the time I found out.

It was his wife who put me in the picture. Eaten up with guilt, I wrote to her, confessing all, but adding, `We didn't mean to kill him.'

In her letter back she dismissed my story. "My poor husband had heart problems," she wrote. "He'd already had one attack. That last one came after news of his brother's accident in a car-crash. You and your friend behaved very wickedly and deserve to feel ashamed, but whatever magic you carried out, I'm afraid he'd have died anyway …"

She's right, I guess… I hope …

I'd like to pass on the news to Shirley, but so much time has passed, and I've no idea where she is now. I wonder if she still thinks she killed Mr Cording by magic, and if she'd be relieved or disappointed to learn that she probably hadn't.

Perhaps one day I'll trace her and find out.

FAMILY MATTERS

This section is reflective rather than violent, and some of the stories have echoes of social attitudes of the past.
Illegitimacy, regarded as so scandalous during the first half of the last century, crops up in three of the stories.
Child abuse appears in another; also, we have the story of a disabled man who fills his lonely hours by chatting to his dead wife.

The last story is futuristic and arguably might be better placed in the first section. However, with so diverse a set of stories, such decisions are hard to make.

THE PORCELAIN DANCER

What shocked Sylvie might have shocked any young girl living back in the nineteen fifties. Social norms and family values have changed since then, and a girl of today might be more shocked by the secrets and lies than by the social disgrace they were meant to cover.

It's funny how an object can trigger off so many memories.

The hat-box in my mother's bedroom takes me way back. I gaze at it, hypnotised by its mottled colour and curved shape as it stands under the dressing-table. It belonged to my grandmother once, as did the bedroom. And today it stands in the same place it had stood fifty years ago, when I was a girl of twelve and first opened it.

Would I ever have found out the truth, I wonder, had I not looked inside that box?

A voice calling from downstairs breaks into my thoughts. "Take something home with you, Sylvie, to remember your mother by. She'd have wanted that." It's John, my stepfather.

"Thanks," I call back. He can't hear me. He's eighty-six now and almost totally deaf. I wonder how he'll cope without my mother's support.

I move over to the dressing-table to choose a memento. Amongst the clutter of porcelain bowls and bottles of scent stands a figurine of a dancer. I pick it up. A cheap souvenir, but pretty. My mother had liked pretty things. I put it down. Not for me.

I look at the hat-box again and feel my eyes glaze over as I relive that time when I had opened it fifty years ago.

It was boredom and curiosity that drove me to it. I knew there were hats inside, old-fashioned straw ones with straggly feathers or ribbons for tying under the chin. No one ever wore them. I'd seen Gran try on one or two before going out, but she'd always end up wearing her old faithfuls - the felt, no-nonsense sort she kept on the wardrobe shelf.

"I'll have a bit of fun with them," I muttered, "It'll be something to do."

I took them out of the hat-box, one by one. That's when I noticed the pool of letters and documents lying at the bottom.

I looked at them in surprise. What were they doing in a hat-box? Had they always been there?

I settled myself on the rug, unfolded a grey, official-looking document and started to read it.

My hand began to shake as the harsh words leapt out at me: `On 21st of June 1939 Miss Beatrice Mason of 25 Mill Road, Treforest, gave birth to a bastard girl …'

I sat staring at the document, heart thumping against my rib-cage. "21st of June. That's my birthday," I murmured. "It's about my mother. And about me."

I couldn't read any more. The writing had grown blurred and my eyes wouldn't focus. *Bastard.* The word had an ugly ring. My best friend, Janet, once told me that if anyone called her brother, Melvyn, a bastard, he would knock him down for insulting his mother.

And *I* was one of those, and had *that* sort of mother. I got angry then. They'd told me lies all along. They'd said my father had died at sea.

Admittedly, I found it odd that my surname was the same as my maternal grandmother's.

"Your mam married a cousin," she explained.

More lies. I'd never trust them again.

I flung the document back in the hatbox, ran downstairs, curled up on the sofa and wept.

My grandmother found me there, her forehead lined with concern.

I said nothing for a minute or two, then blurted out, "I looked in the hat-box. I know everything."

She stared at me, frowning. "Hatbox?" Then the penny seemed to drop. She whitened. "You had no business poking about in there."

That was all she said. No explanation. No move to comfort me. I watched her turn and scurry out.

Five minutes later, she was back, followed by our next door neighbour.

She spoke without meeting my eye. "Here's Mrs Davies, Sylvie, to have a talk with you. She knows all about it." She hurried out again, leaving her neighbour to deal with the problem.

Mrs Davies plonked herself on a nearby chair and leaned towards me, her double-chin wobbling as she talked. "There, there, Sylvie, love. It's not the end of the world," she began, her voice rough, like gravel. "Your father came from a respectable family."

"Why didn't they tell me the truth?" I blubbed.

"They thought it was for the best." Mrs Davies drew from her pinafore-pocket a handkerchief smothered in eucalyptus and passed it to me. "Dry your eyes now. No need to feel ashamed. After all, it's not *your* fault. That's what I tell our Nellie, and anyone else who points the finger."

So people pointed the finger. Worse and worse. "Then everybody knows?" I faltered.

"No, no. Not everyone. Only a few of us living here in this street."

I hate myself for it now but I began to despise my mother. My only excuse is being a child of my time, when a girl who 'got herself in trouble' was rated just a step or two up from the criminal classes. She's brought shame on herself and on me, I whinged.

I yearned to be like other children. In the forties and fifties, that meant having two parents, married to each other, and a brother or sister, all living in a nice, tidy family.

On the other hand, being different made me feel kind of *special*. Perhaps my father was handsome, capable, talented, I thought, just like the fathers in story-books. Maybe he was cleverer than my quiet, slow mother who seemed to be frightened of everything and good at nothing.

I longed to meet him.

"You can't," Gran said, pushing back a wisp of hair straying from her bun. "He's far away. In London, I think." She tightened her lips.

"Forget about him," Aunt Hilda snapped, her eyes flashing. "He let your mother down. And he's a no-good drunk."

"It's not true," I wailed.

My mother said nothing. She went about the house, cleaning, dusting, a bleak expression on her face. I could almost feel her heart sinking.

But there was no let-up in my coldness towards her. For weeks I gave her hardly a smile or a friendly word.

I cringe now when I recall the shabby, indifferent way I behaved towards her, probably driving her self-esteem even lower than it already was.

I continued to fantasize about my father. Perhaps he wasn't in London, as my grandmother supposed. Maybe he was here in my home-town. Often, as I walked along the streets, I'd find myself scanning middle-aged men, wondering if one of them could be my father. If he were bald, fat or loud-mouthed, I'd mentally shake my head. It couldn't be him. If, on the other hand, he looked elegant, clever, and a cut above the others, I'd smile and think, perhaps he's the one.

A year or so later, my mother married. I didn't care for my stepfather, John. He was quiet and ordinary, like my mother, and he worked in the pit. There weren't any parents like that in the books I read. Years later, I came to realise I read the wrong sorts of books. I should have read more Dickens or Hardy and less Enid Blyton. I moved into my grandmother's rooms on the ground floor, more determined than ever to track down my father.

I felt sure Aunt Hilda knew of his whereabouts. I pestered her till she weakened. She flung up her hands. "Okay, if you're that keen, I'll arrange something. But on your own head be it."

She frowned and went on, "He's left London, and his wife. Typical. And he's back down here, like a bad penny."

My heart began to thump. Being back down here wasn't exactly a good omen. The smart ones usually left and they didn't come back. Still, you never know. I crossed my fingers.

We met in a café, further up the valley, with blue plastic covers on the tables and a strong smell of hot pies. I was too excited to eat, and made do with a lemonade.

I sat there sipping it, enjoying its frothy tang, and staring curiously at the man who was my father. He's not bad-looking, I decided. Not bald or fat. And he doesn't put *Brylcream* in his hair.

He seemed to shrink under my gaze. He uttered an awkward `Well, well ...' and made a business of adjusting his tie. At last, he said, haltingly, "I've often wondered about you, and - er - how you were getting on." He fumbled in his pocket. "And - I've brought you a present."

Well, that was a good start. He held out a wrist watch. I gave a squeal of delight. I'd never had a wrist-watch before.

I asked him what he did. Being the little snob I was, I prayed he wasn't a labourer, or working down the pit.

He didn't answer straight away but rummaged inside his jacket for a cigarette. I noticed his hand tremble as he lit it. After a few drags, he appeared to relax.

"What do you do?" I asked again.

He made a vague gesture with his fingers. "Oh, this and that. I'm a bit of a butterfly. Not like the rest of the family. There were seven of us, you know." He gave a wry smile. "I was the black sheep"

He went into a long spiel about his brothers and sisters. "Most of them went to University," he told me.

"Your Uncle Arthur went to Oxford. Dan became a doctor, and your Aunt Glenys, a dress designer. My brother, Llewellyn, went into business. He owns most of the street you live in."

I felt a thrill of satisfaction. So I had successful relatives. Great.

"But what about you?"

He paused again. "I played in a band once."

"So you're a musician. That's nice."

"And I've been a carpenter. And an insurance clerk ..." He ticked them off on his fingers.

We talked some more. Finally, he paid the bill and gave me an awkward kiss before parting.

I met him several times after that. We never bonded though. I was never able to call him *Dad*.

My aunt was right about his drinking. Almost every time I called I'd find him with a beer in front of him, his speech slurred and his movements unsteady. And with his drunkenness came a mean-spiritedness and a tendency to growl and snap about some trifling letdown he'd suffered in the past.

As my disappointment grew, so our meetings got fewer, until soon they ceased altogether.

I didn't tell Aunt Hilda. I know what she'd have said.

My stepfather calling from below brings an end to my reverie. "Sylvie, are you okay? They're all asking about you down here."

"Coming."

I think again about my mother and her crushed, pushed-aside life, the presents she sent for my birthday, that she couldn't afford, her mild manner towards me, in spite of my cold looks and my slights. I did try to make amends later on, but things were never the same.

And now she's gone.

My reminiscences bring a lump to my throat, and I cry at last. She could have given me up. I wouldn't have blamed her. They were hard on unmarried mothers in those days.

I wipe my eyes. I must join the others. But first there's something I'd like to do.

I cross to the dressing-table and pick up the porcelain dancer from the top. As I gaze at the figurine, it seems to let out a strange, unearthly glow. I catch my breath and gaze a while longer.

Then, gently, and with a lighter heart, I slip it in my handbag and go downstairs.

FATHERLY FEELINGS

The setting is a Welsh mining valley in the 1990s. There are few coal mines left and not many chapels in this once religious community. But one thing that hasn't died is the people's love of singing.

Ivor woke with a grunt as the church bells in his dream turned into the daunting ring of his alarm clock. Damn! He had to get up. What the devil for? That was the question. *Duw Mawr*! His memory was going. Old age didn't come by itself.

He raised himself slowly onto his elbows. A clatter of dishes from below in the kitchen reminded him that his wife, Blodwen, was already up and doing the breakfast. He'd better shift himself, or there'd be trouble.

He squeezed his eyes open, felt for his glasses on the bedside table and switched on the lamp. The first thing he noticed was his best suit hanging over the wardrobe door. That's when he remembered. Of course. It was Mair's big day. His younger daughter was singing solo at the *Cymanfa Gani,* held in Moriah chapel this morning, and he and Blod were going to hear her.

He eased himself to the edge of the bed. Mair had sung like a bird as a young girl, he mused, even winning prizes at the Eisteddfod. The whole of the Rhondda had heard of Mair the Voice.

He drew aside the bedclothes and tottered to his feet. He didn't feel so bright now he was up. His head was beginning to spin and he had a weird, dazed sort of feeling, as though he'd pass out, if he wasn't careful. Was he getting one of his turns?

He sank down on the bed again and, taking a deep breath, clutched the edge of the mattress.

"Ivor, time to get up!" his wife called from the stairs. There was a pause. Then, "You haven't forgotten our Mair's singing today, I hope. You ought to be proud of her, going back to it again, after all those years bringing up a family. Come on now. No excuses."

Ivor straightened, murmuring, "I *am* bloody well proud of her." He clenched his jaw. "And this time, I'll *show* it, even if it kills me."

He gritted his teeth and pulled himself up, clutching a corner of the bedside chest. Made it.

He stumbled to the wash-room, clinging to walls and bits of furniture as he went. He was doing fine. Whatever happened, he'd go. He wouldn't let Mair down. Not this time.

He'd done enough of that in the past. Not once when she was a child had he gone to hear her sing. Not always his fault. He was usually on the wrong shift at the time, and the others at the pit were never keen to do a swap. But he knew Mair saw things differently. She was sure that had her sister, Joan, been the singer, he'd have found *some* way of getting to see her.

And she was right. No use denying it. Ivor wiped his hands on the nearest towel and sighed. Joan had always been his favourite, plump, easy-going Joan who couldn't sing a note, but knocked spots off Mair at school.

He limped his way back to the bedroom and began to dress.

"Ivor! You up yet?" his wife called from the stairs. "Your breakfast's ready."

"Okay, okay." Ivor pushed a comb through what was left of his hair. "Well, never mind, Mair, *bach*," he murmured. "Today, I'll be there to support you. Even if you make a mess of things, I'll pat you on the back and I'll say, `Well done, *Cariad*, your dad's proud of you'."

The sound of a car drawing up outside broke into his thoughts. Joan. Coming to collect them.

Soon he heard voices in the passage.

"I bet the old so-and-so's still in bed," came Blod's voice. "I set the alarm too, *and* called him. Ivor, are you up yet?"

"Don't worry, Mam, he'll be up," Joan said, calmly. "He won't miss hearing Mair sing. Not now, after all these years."

"I'm not so sure. He never did care for our Mair the way a father should. Remember those hard smacks he gave her that time? I know she could be a little devil, but she was only eight."

"Well, she *did* call Auntie May a daft old bat." Joan laughed. "And, smacking or no, she still wouldn't apologise. Say what you like, our Mair had guts, even then."

They began to climb the stairs, Blod huffing and snorting, "All your father cared about in them days was working for the Communist party, and getting into politics. A lot of good it did him. He only ended up in the pit, same as his butties!"

"Well, there *were* only the pits round here then. Now, even they've gone. Everything's changed."

"Everything, except your father," Blod grumbled.

"After all these years, he's still an old communist. He'd have tried converting Margaret Thatcher, given the chance."

The bedroom door burst open. "Ivor," came Blod's anxious voice. Then, "Oh, you're ready. I hope you had a good wash."

"There's smart you're looking, Dad," said Joan. "You'll have all the women at the *Dog and Muffler* chasing you tonight, in that suit."

Ivor poked at his jacket with a contemptuous thumb. "I'm not wearing this at the Club," he said. "I'm out of it, soon as the show's over."

A quick breakfast, a five minute drive to Dunraven Street and they were standing outside Moriah Chapel.

Ivor gazed pensively at the tired, stone building with its arched entrance. Once, he reflected, there were chapels like this all over the Valleys. Now they were almost as rare as the coal pits. Not that he missed them. He'd never been a chapel-goer, like Blod. He'd miss the mountains though, if they, somehow, disappeared. The mountains were *home*. They hugged the valleys, as mothers hugged their children. Even behind this ugly old building, you could see the comforting outlines of mountain slopes.

He turned his gaze to the people thronging the chapel entrance.

Blod nudged him. "Look, there's Mrs Jones the Post. And we thought she was dead." She looked around her in wonder. "*Duw, Duw*! It's crowded. Just like it used to be in the old days." She gave a nostalgic sigh.

"I bet they've only come to hear Mair sing," Joan said. "The older ones will remember her as a girl, and the lovely voice she had."

They made their way upstairs to the main gallery, and settled themselves in the second row, facing the pulpit. Ivor winced as he sat down. The wooden seat felt hard as a rock beneath his scraggy behind. He sniffed. There was a funny smell too. What was it? Damp?

He rubbed his eyes. He still felt odd. The garish picture above the pulpit, of Christ being baptised by John, seemed to lurch towards him and then to recede and disintegrate in the most disconcerting way. He wished that John the Baptist wouldn't keep changing into Karl Marx and Christ into Margaret Thatcher. He wasn't a religious man but still had an uneasy feeling that there was something blasphemous about the changes he kept seeing in the picture. He blinked. He must have his eyes tested. Maybe he had cataracts.

He felt an elbow nudging him in the ribs. With relief he turned away from the picture.

"There's our Mair, Dad," whispered Joan. "See her in the front row of the choir? Don't she look nice?"

Ivor turned his head to the left gallery where Mair sat with the other choristers, studying her song-sheets. Her face was chalky-white.

"She's nervous," muttered Ivor.

"If she's as nervous as I am, God help her," Joan said, taking her father's hand for support.

"It was different when she was a girl," she went on. "We knew then she'd be good. But now, after all these years ... God, I feel sick."

Blodwen leaned towards her. "Don't worry, Joan, *bach*. Mair will be all right." She lowered her voice. "She told me yesterday she's been having singing lessons for the last six months. Kept it all a secret till now, bless her heart."

Ivor felt a warm glow sweep through him. He'd encourage her from now on, show her some interest and affection for once in his life. Then the dizziness started again and the picture of John baptising Christ began to waver and blur, before receding into the distance.

Soon Blod was helping him to his feet for the first hymn. He swayed a little as he stood sharing Blod's hymn-book. This was the boring part

He sat uncomfortably through two Welsh songs sung by the choir, dozed through the preacher's sermon and another choral piece. At last, Joan clutched at his arm. It was Mair's turn to sing. The piece was *Ave Maria*.

Right from the first few notes, everyone sat quite still, lips parted, thrilling in the pure sounds flowing effortlessly from the pale woman's mouth.

Ivor felt a lump come to his throat. Voice like an angel, he said to himself. Tears moistened his eyes. Joan caught hold of his hand and squeezed it.

Mair hit the top note with ease then, without hitch or tremor, brought the song to its final *Amen*.

There was first an awed silence, followed by an outbreak of appreciative grunts and murmurs. She had moved the whole congregation.

One more hymn and the service was at an end. People began to filter out or talk in groups. Ivor watched Mair. She was leaving her seat, and people were stopping to shake hands and congratulate her. He saw a grey-haired, distinguished-looking man grasp her arm.

"That's Arthur Phillips," Blod whispered, "If anyone can do anything for our Mair, he can."

Ivor's heart began to beat, madly. Mair was going to have a future. She wasn't going to vegetate in comfortable squalor, like him and Blod. He must go and see her. Now. Make amends.

He got up. But then came that dizzy feeling again, with the whole chapel seeming to sway forwards and backwards, forwards and backwards. The picture behind the pulpit made no sense now, just blotches of colour.

He fell back in his seat.

Mair, smiling and triumphant, was already making her way towards them. "Well, did you enjoy it?" She looked hard at Ivor. "What's the matter, Dad? Been at the whisky already?"

Ivor tried again to stand up, supporting himself on the seat in front. He mouthed the words, "I'm proud of you, Mair, *bach*." But no sound came out, just a desperate movement of his lips.

Mair frowned and turned to her mother. "What's he on about?"

"Praising you for your singing, I expect."

"Huh, that'll be the day. I gave up trying to please Dad a long time ago."

Ivor opened and closed his mouth as though struggling for air. At last, with a mighty effort, he gasped out, "Well done, Mair!"

Mair didn't hear. She had already moved away and was chatting to Dr and Mrs Evans.

Ivor let out a choking sound, clutched at his chest, then flopped into his seat.

"What's wrong, Dad? God, look at him, Mam. He looks awful. I'll go and get Dr Evans." Joan jumped up and scurried to the end of the row to summon the doctor.

Blodwen scanned her husband's face with anxious eyes. "Ivor, Ivor, what's the matter with you? Speak to me!"

But he said nothing. His eyes were glazed and a drop of blood dribbled from his mouth. He crumpled forward in his seat.

Ivor had said his last words.

REPLAY

The phone is resting on the coffee table in front of me. "Go on, pick it up," I tell myself. "It's easy enough."

I stretch out a hand but withdraw it again.

Wrong. It's not easy. Nothing is easy these days. Not since that Saturday two weeks ago when my daughter, Rachel, appeared unexpectedly at the back door.

I lean back on the sofa, reliving that day.

I'd been in the kitchen, frying omelettes for me and Mike, when she arrived, face flushed, eyes sparkling.

"You look as if you've just had a win on the horses, love," Mike said, lowering his paper.

"Better than that, Dad." She gave him a quick kiss. "It's great news. I'm just off to meet Luke. We're going to Dino's for lunch to celebrate."

I left the omelettes for a moment and smiled across at her. They've decided to get married, I thought. About time Rachel settled down. She'd been so focussed on her job at the lab she'd given little time to serious relationships. But now there was Luke... A picture of her in a satin wedding-dress, surrounded by bouquets of flowers, flew into my mind. She hadn't known Luke that long but he seemed a decent enough young man.

The news, when it came, wasn't what I expected.

"I'm pregnant," she announced.

"What?" I sank down on a chair while the omelettes fizzed and dried in the pan. "Couldn't you have waited till you were married?" I could hear my voice harden and feel a frown appear between my eyes. "Surely, Rachel, you've been taking precautions?"

"I was, but then I stopped." She turned to me, earnestly. "I'm nearly thirty-seven, Mum. I might be past child-bearing if I wait for marriage."

"But why do you have to wait? You don't want an illegitimate child, surely?"

Rachel rolled her eyes. "Honestly, Mum, you sound as if we're still in the Victorian era. Nobody cares about that sort of thing any more."

I let her remark wash over me. I'm used to being teased about my old-fashioned values. "So when are you going to get married? Soon, I hope." I sighed. There wouldn't be time to prepare the sort of wedding I'd had in mind.

She looked away a moment and pretended to take great interest in the potted plant on the window sill. At last she said, "We haven't decided yet, but it won't be for about a year."

I gasped, "A year!"

She shrugged and fiddled with a leaf. "I'm in no hurry. Anyway, Luke won't be free to marry till then." She lowered her eyes. "That's when his divorce comes through."

I almost lost my breath at that point. "You mean Luke is already married?" I flung my arms into the air. "Why didn't you tell us? We're your parents, for heaven's sake. We have a right to know."

"Yes. And I guessed what your reaction would be. Besides, it's not your problem." She turned and gave me a defiant look. "I'm a grown woman, Mum. I have my own home, my own life, and I make my own decisions. That's what we agreed when I moved out those years ago. Remember?"

I got up and turned off the gas under the charred remains of omelette. Yes, I remembered our agreement, and I know I shouldn't interfere. But, although Rachel's in her thirties now, I still see her as my little girl, needing protection. Hence my angry response: "He can't be much of a man, leaving his wife for another woman," I snorted, "and then making her pregnant."

"Leave it, Jess!" Mike slapped his paper down on the table. "I'm sure Rachel knows what she's doing."

"She knows nothing." I snatched the pan off the hob and banged it down on the worktop. "She's just tying a noose around her neck. And I can't do anything to stop her."

Rachel sprang forward. "I knew you'd take it like this. That's why I didn't tell you. You're a prude, Mum, still living in the fifties. And you've no reason to be. *You're* no angel."

I stood gaping at her as she flounced to the door.

"Luke is a good man, and I won't have anything said against him. And he didn't leave his wife for me. He was already separated when we met." She opened the door, then turned to face me, eyes glistening with disappointed tears. "I thought you'd be thrilled to hear you were going to have a grandchild." She made a choking sound in her throat and murmured, "Dream on, Rachel."

I subsided as I heard the pain in her voice. I would have gone after her, but Mike laid a restraining hand on my arm as she slammed out of the house.

I knew I hadn't handled the situation well but then I've never really known how to handle Rachel. I've never felt I quite measured up to her expectations of me as a mother.

I *was* thrilled at the thought of having a grandchild. But not out of wedlock. I know ideas have changed since I was a girl. But there were still downsides to being a single mother. My mind whirled with all the possibilities as I turned to Mike. "Suppose he leaves her, stranded with a baby, all on her own. It's hard for single mothers, having to juggle a job with child care and housekeeping, struggling to pay bills."

I thought of an article I'd read earlier in the week. "You hear of fatherless children growing up wild, turning to crime and drugs …"

"That can happen to children with *two* parents. And even couples who are married often split up. There aren't any guarantees." He came over and hugged me. "Rachel is sensible and well organised. I'm sure she knows how to look after herself."

"If she'd been sensible, she wouldn't have got involved with a married man," I retorted. "If he's left his wife, he can leave her too."

He shrugged. "There might have been good reasons for their separating."

I sighed and shook my head. "Who's to say he won't change his mind and go back to his wife in six months time or find someone else who's not burdened with a baby? Sometimes a woman gets pregnant and off the man goes."

Mike tightened his hold on me reassuringly. "You're still living in the past, love. Rachel's life is not your life. Luke seems a reliable sort. I don't think he'll leave her in the lurch."

I wanted to believe that. That's why I decided to go and see him myself and have a chat.

He was dressed in paint-stained overalls when I arrived. There were newspapers littering the floor with pots of paint and brushes around.

"Hullo, Jen. This is a surprise." His manner was cool.

It was clear Rachel had told him about our meeting the day before. He drew a chair forward for me to sit down, then rested his paintbrush over a pot of white paint.

"I'm not staying," I said, quickly. "I came because I'm worried about Rachel."

"Why? Because she's pregnant? Aren't you looking forward to having your first grandchild?"

"I would be, if she were married. But you've got a wife already, I hear. That's no security for my daughter or my grandchild."

"I'll be free to marry Rachel in eighteen months."

I frowned. "A lot can happen in eighteen months."

He spun round. "Why do you think I'm decorating this place? To make it into a home for Rachel and the child she's carrying." He knelt down on the floor and looked hard at me. "This isn't a replay of your life, Jen. Just because some fellow made you pregnant years ago then waltzed off back to the wife you didn't know about, doesn't mean I'm going to do the same."

His words were like a punch in the stomach. How did he know about that? I hadn't told anyone except Mike whom I'd met years afterwards. Even my parents had known nothing. I'd slunk away from home, too ashamed to tell them. I felt my cheeks burn at the memory.

Luke must have seen the look on my face. He softened his voice. "Sorry, Jen. Rachel knew, I'm afraid. She discovered some letters in an old tin box up in your loft. And a birth certificate and photograph of the little boy you gave up for adoption. David, wasn't it?" He shook his head. "It must have been hell for you."

My mind flew back to the horror of that time: the weeks at the home for unmarried mothers, the pressure to let the baby go, so he'd be brought up in a proper home with loving parents able to support him, the trauma at the time of parting. It had been hell all right.

I thought of Martin, the man who had claimed to love me, but who promptly disappeared on hearing of my pregnancy. It wasn't until that last meeting that he told me about his wife.

My mind skipped forward to the present. And Rachel knew about it, I thought, bitterly, and told Luke. How could she? I felt again the shame of those old days of being an unmarried woman and pregnant.

"Rachel never said anything," I muttered, looking at the floor. "All these years, and she never said a thing."

"Perhaps she thought you'd prefer to keep it private."

"She told *you*." I was near to tears now, tears of humiliation. "He did promise to marry me," I said at last. "And I, like a fool, believed him." I got up, my lips pursed. "I don't want that happening to Rachel."

He stepped forward and took my arm, earnestly. "Jen, I'd marry her tomorrow, if I could. But we have to wait a while. You know that."

"Yes. And anything might happen in the meantime. You might go back to your wife."

He tightened his hold on my arm. "Or Rachel might tire of me, or meet someone else. Anything might happen, as you say." He swung me round to face him. "Do you think that having a ring on your finger takes away all risk, when one in three marriages break up?" His face darkened. "You can't go on running Rachel's life for her. She's fed up with it. That's why she left home those years ago, to escape your control."

I shook off his hand, enraged. "Well at least she had a home, and loving parents. I'm not at all sure that my grandchild will get that."

Without saying another word, I picked up my handbag and left.

That had been two weeks ago. I have no idea what's happening now. I expect Luke has told Rachel about my disastrous visit. Perhaps by this time they are living happily together in Luke's house.

It's been a long two weeks, and I've been doing a lot of thinking. That's why I have to make this call. I'll assume they're at Luke's place and ring there. It doesn't matter who answers. I need to speak to them both.

I need to tell Rachel I'm sorry for trying to run her life in the past instead of allowing her to make her own choices and her own mistakes.

And I need to apologise to Luke for making unfair assumptions about him, based on a single experience of my own. I don't know what went wrong between him and his wife but I dare say he wasn't wholly to blame. Underneath I think he's a decent man who genuinely loves my daughter.

And I need to tell them both that, whatever I might have thought or said, I'm thrilled at having my first grandchild.

Suddenly, it's easy. I take a deep breath and pick up the phone.

OMISSION OF TRUTH

Sarah Clark sat up, ears pricked. Was she imagining things, or was there something going on in the girls' cloakroom? She pushed aside the pile of Year 3 exercise books and got up. It couldn't be any of the children, she decided, as she stepped out of the classroom. They'd left for home some time ago. And there weren't any other teachers in this separate area they called the *hut.*

As soon as she reached the cloakroom, she could hear it clearly. Someone crying in one of the cubicles. A child.

Startled, she knocked at the door. "Hullo?"

The sobs quietened, turned to whimpers, then stopped.

She knocked again. "Who's in there? Open the door, please."

A few moments elapsed. She heard a click. Then the door opened and out crept the forlorn little figure of Sophie Dunne, shoulders hunched, eyes focussed on the ground. Her face was red and smudged with tears.

"Why, Sophie!" Sarah drew the child to her, smoothing damp strands of hair away from her face. "What's wrong? Are you hurt?"

She shook her head.

"Why haven't you gone home, like the others?" Sarah led her to the wash-basin and murmured, "Let's get that face washed. We can talk while I'm driving you home. It's very late."

Sophie wriggled away and began to whimper again. "I - I don't w-want to go home."

Sarah's heart gave a lurch. The child looked scared stiff. "Why not, Sophie?"

"I f-fell down home-time and r-ripped my new cardigan. Look." She pointed to a tear below the pocket. "I got it dirty too. Mum'll kill me. She don't like dirt."

She pressed her hands against her eyes and burst into sobs again.

Sarah felt her own eyes mist up. Poor little kid. Was she so afraid of a scolding that she couldn't face going home?

She sighed. She'd worried about Sophie ever since the child had joined the school two months before. The family, she learned, had moved from Hertfordshire, the county she herself had grown up in. But Sophie was finding it hard to adjust. Sarah had often noticed her staring into space, biting her nails or twisting strands of hair round her fingers. And she'd made few friends at her new school.

"It's all right, dear, don't cry. I'll see your Mum and explain."

She seemed to relax.

Relieved, Sarah washed and dried Sophie's face, checked her address, then ushered her to the car.

A five minute drive brought them to a row of terraced houses in a cul-de-sac.

"You said you'd have a word with Mum," Sophie reminded her.

"I haven't forgotten." Sarah smiled and rang the doorbell.

Soon, the door opened, letting out a strong whiff of floor polish. Mrs Dunne was certainly big on cleanliness, Sarah thought. She looked at the woman facing her. She was heavily-built, in her thirties, with frizzy blonde hair and small, bad-tempered mouth. She looked harder. There was something familiar about her face. Had they met before?

She gave Sarah no more than a cursory glance and a quick thank you before grabbing Sophie by the arm and hauling her in.

"She's terribly upset," Sarah began.

"So am I," Mrs Dunne snapped and, without a second glance at Sarah, shut the door in her face.

Sarah gaped at the closed door. She heard Mrs Dunne yelling at Sophie from the passage. "Why are so late getting home, you little toe-rag? And look at that new cardigan! It's filthy."

There came the sound of hard slaps, followed by a shriek from Sophie. "That's right, cry!" Mrs Dunne bawled. "You'll cry even harder when I get hold of my clothes brush."

Frozen to the doorstep, Sarah heard Sophie wailing and pleading. Soon, a door slammed from somewhere inside, muffling the sounds. Sarah stood rigid a moment. Then her emotions blazed into action. She'd put a stop this. Now. She rang the bell again. Hard. Rattled on the door with her fist.

No answer. She tried once more. Still no answer.

She gave up and returned to the car, her inside churning.

Tomorrow, she'd see Ralph Bird, the Head, and tell him about it. Those were no ordinary slaps she had heard. They'd echoed through the house.

The possibility that Sophie might be abused like that, day after day, sent a shudder up her spine.

When Sophie turned up for school the following morning, Sarah's worst fears seemed to be confirmed. The child had a bruise running down her left cheek and another on her arm.

She gave a gasp. "Sophie, what happened?"

"I fell off a swing," Sophie mumbled.

The rest of the class stared at her.

"She's always having accidents, Miss," piped up Jane Franks, one of the girls at Sophie's table.

Sarah stiffened. She remembered now the other times when Sophie had turned up with bruises. She's accident-prone she'd thought. Child abuse hadn't occurred to her. "You'd better stay in playtime, Sophie," she said, "in case you fall again."

During the break that morning, she strode to the head's office, ready to voice her suspicions.

"It's all right, Sarah. Mrs Dunne's already explained." Ralph Bird looked up from a pile of reports and took a sip of coffee. "Sophie fell off her swing, apparently. It sounded genuine enough."

His eyebrows twitched with impatience as Sarah went into detail. "Are you sure you're not making mountains out of molehills, Sarah? Even if you did hear Sophie being smacked, that's not enough reason to link it to her bruises."

"Her mother *beats* her, Ralph. Really hard. Yesterday, she was too scared to go home. I'm worried about these so-called accidents. Perhaps I should contact a social worker."

Ralph shrugged. "It's up to you. But make sure you're right. We don't want any trouble."

"Don't worry, I'll make sure." Sarah pursed her lips as she returned to the classroom. Mountains out of molehills indeed, she thought, angrily. Ralph Bird was too laid-back by half.

She'd do without her coffee in the staffroom this morning and talk to Sophie instead.

She hurried back to the classroom where the girl sat alone reading.

"I'm worried about those bruises, Sophie," she began. "How exactly did you get them?"

Sophie looked up warily from her book. "I told you, Miss. I fell off a swing."

"How? Were you going too high?"

Sophie frowned. "I dunno, Miss." She evaded Sarah's eyes and turned to her book.

She was fibbing. Sarah could tell. She tried again. "Your mum was cross with you yesterday. She smacked you, didn't she?"

"No, she didn't do nothin'." She looked up at Sarah, anxiety flooding her face.

"Sophie, I *heard* her. Tell me the truth, please. Did your mum give you those bruises?"

Tears began to fall. At last she gave a reluctant nod. "I'm not supposed to say, but Mum whacked me with the clothes-brush, 'cause of my cardigan. After supper, I asked to phone Daddy. Mum got really mad then and whacked me again." She dabbed at her tears. "Daddy's gone," she explained.

Sarah handed her a tissue from the box on her desk. It was unbelievable. Hitting a child because she wanted to talk to her father!

"I'd better have a word with your mum."

"You mustn't say I told you." A frown creased her forehead.

"I won't, I promise."

Before leaving school that day, Sarah looked up Mrs Dunne's number and phoned her.

"I'm concerned about Sophie," she said, "Could I visit you this evening for a chat?"

"Okay. But not while the soaps are on." Her voice sharpened. "Sophie hasn't been playing you up, I hope?"

"Not at all."

"You're lucky then. The little devil plays me up all the time."

Sarah got there at six. Mrs Dunne didn't invite her in, but stood on the doorstep, her large frame swathed in a blue kaftan, hair tied in a bunch on the top of her head. Where *had* she seen her before?

"I'm worried about these accidents Sophie keeps having," Sarah began.

"Well don't. She's a *dream*, like her father. Never looks where she's going." She rolled her eyes.

Sarah paused and took a deep breath. "I think she's being abused."

Sophie's mother stepped back, mouth dropping open. "Who by?" she demanded.

Sarah looked her straight in the eye. "By *you*, Mrs Dunne. I was outside your door yesterday and heard that terrible beating you gave her. I was appalled."

Mrs Dunne shot forward, her face twisted into a look of rage. She clenched a fist. "Don't you tell me how to discipline my child, you bossy, interfering bitch!"

Sarah stood her ground. "You bruised her, Mrs Dunne. That's *abuse*, not discipline."

Mrs Dunne peered at Sarah through narrowed eyes. Then a flicker of a smile played at the corners of her mouth. "And what are you going to do about it?"

"I'm going to report you and see that you're put under supervision."

"I don't think so." Her smile widened. "Not unless you want the boot." A look of triumph crossed her face. "You see, my love, I know all about you. I know what you and your pals at Lonsdale School got up to on Saturdays. I'd already left, but it was all in the Echo. Remember? Does old Bird know that you're a *thief*?"

Sarah's heart almost missed a beat. Of course. That's where they'd met before. At Lonsdale School. She'd put on weight over the years, and she'd bleached her hair, but she was still the same bully. And she wouldn't hesitate at resorting to blackmail!

Sarah's mind flashed back to her last year at school. She'd got in with the popular Jarvis set. A big mistake. "Let's go shop-lifting again, for a bit of fun," one of them suggested. When she shrank back in horror, they sniggered and called her a wimp. So she tagged along, legs like jelly, heart slamming against her chest. She didn't steal anything herself. Nonetheless, when the store detective caught them, a silk scarf was found in her bag, planted by one of the others.

She flushed at the memory. They'd got themselves police records. And when she'd filled in her teaching application those years ago, she'd not mentioned it, and nobody had made enquiries.

A hoarse chuckle from Mrs Dunne disrupted her thoughts. "You kept it quiet, didn't you? You knew they wouldn't have taken on a thief to teach their kids."

Sarah, trying to ignore the knot in her stomach, drew herself up straight. "You can make any accusations you like, Mrs Dunne, but if you harm Sophie again, I'll not hesitate to report you."

"And if you do, my love, I'll not hesitate to get you chucked out of Redwood School." She laughed and slammed the door.

Sarah turned away, biting her lip. Her heart was still pounding from the interview as she drove home. What was she going to do? Report Mrs Dunne, and risk losing her job? She felt a throbbing at her temples. Could she face giving up teaching? The very idea brought tears to her eyes.

Teaching had become her life. Whatever the headaches and heartaches of the work, she could think of nothing else that made her feel so complete.

She argued with herself as she drove home. If I report Mrs Dunne, she reflected, Sophie might get to live with her father. But she *could* end up going into care. Hardly the best of situations. And what happens to me?

Unease gnawed at her stomach as she pondered on the consequences. I'll probably be hauled before some panel, she thought. They might take my age into account. I was only seventeen after all. And I'm a good teacher. But suppose they don't …

She decided to wait. She'd keep a watchful eye on Sophie and hope for the best.

Nothing happened for a couple of weeks. Relief flooded her. Sophie seemed happier, less anxious. She chatted to Sarah. "I saw Daddy and Auntie Lisa at the weekend," she said, coming up to Sarah's desk before play time. "They're getting married." Her eyes sparkled. "Auntie Lisa reads me stories."

"Do you see them often?" Sarah asked.

Her face clouded. "No. Mum don't like them coming for me. She don't trust them."

So, her father was with another woman. No wonder her mother was fed-up. Still, that was no excuse for taking her feelings out on a child.

At least, Sarah thought, there had been no `accidents' for a while, and Sophie was looking more cheerful. Perhaps her warning to Mrs Dunne had had some effect.

If it had, it didn't last.

Early the following week, when Sophie arrived at school, Sarah could see that something was wrong. Her face was pale and there was a stiffness in her movements. Later that morning, she happened to rest her hand on the child's back while marking her work. Sophie winced at her touch and let out a cry of pain.

Sarah stepped back in alarm. Another *accident*?

That afternoon, her suspicions were confirmed. When Sophie reluctantly changed for PE, she revealed to Sarah a back full of cuts and bruises. At the end of the day, she blurted out the truth. "I tried to run away to Dad and Auntie Lisa," she sobbed, "But Mum caught me. She went mad."

Sarah felt a heavy, burning sensation in her chest.

No more waiting, she murmured to herself. No more fretting about losing her job. She was an adult.

And she'd survive, whatever the outcome. A child was a different matter.

She knew then what she had to do.

She rummaged in her handbag for her address-book, got out her mobile and began to dial.

A QUESTION OF DEGREE

Ruth shifted from one foot to the other as she faced her parents at the front door. This wasn't going to be an easy homecoming.

"Where in heaven's name have you been, Ruth?" She saw her father's eyebrows knot, as he bent down for her suitcase and wheeled it into the hall. "We've phoned you, texted you, but there's been no answer."

"Yes, darling, we were so worried." Her mother patted her new hair-do before giving her daughter a hug. "We've hardly heard from you since Christmas. I know you've been studying hard and taking jobs in the holidays. But we expected you home straight after your finals."

Ruth sighed. "D'you mind if we talk about it later. I'm dog-tired, and I'd love a cup of tea."

She stepped into the hall with its familiar smell of floor-polish, slung her jacket on a hook, then followed her mother into the drawing-room where she sank down on the sofa and closed her eyes.

"I was about to take some scones from the oven," her mother said. She bustled into the kitchen, skirt rustling, heels clicking on the polished floor.

No slopping around the house in jeans and old slippers for Mother, Ruth thought, with a wry smile. You never knew who might call.

She listened to cups clinking, cupboards opening, and later, her father's footsteps thudding down the stairs. In a moment, she thought, they'll be sitting here, firing questions at me. She had her answers ready.

She'd been rehearsing them on the train and afterwards in the taxi.

She wondered how they'd react, these go-ahead, socially active parents of hers with their concerns about achievement and place in the community. She chewed her lip. They'd be hurt, angry. Could she go through with it? She squared her shoulders. She *had* to. It was the only way.

Her father strode in. He lowered his tall, angular frame into the upholstered chair opposite her, and leaned forward. "Well, Ruth, what's the news about your exams? We expected you to phone us days ago when your results were in. Perhaps you were too busy celebrating. Never mind." He brushed the air with his hands. "You're here now. How did you do?"

"Yes, darling, we're dying to know." An aroma of hot pastry filled the room as her mother came in laden with tea and scones. "Why didn't you phone?" She handed Ruth her tea, a hurt little smile hovering on her face.

Ruth glanced at her father. The frown had gone now, and his brown eyes glinted with eagerness. "There's an opening at my firm for a research assistant, Ruth. With a good honours degree, the job's yours." He stretched out his arms, palms upward.

Ruth paused to sip her tea, finding comfort in its hot sweetness. "Thanks, Dad, but no thanks. I've other plans."

She noticed him stiffen, his eyebrows arch. "Plans? What plans?"

Ruth felt a stab of anger. Was he still trying to control her? "My *own* plans. I do have them from time to time.

Anyway, there's that job I took last month."

"That was only temporary, wasn't it, dear? Something to tide you over till your results came out?" Her mother's smile was anxious. "You can't do a *gardening* job for the rest of your life. Not with a degree in Economics."

She glanced at her husband for support. His mouth tightened. "I dare say it's Ruth's latest beau – Steve or whatever his name is – who's behind the idea."

Ruth took a fierce bite of her scone. Did they think she had no mind of her own? If Steve had taught her anything, it was to be her *own person*. "Don't let anyone push you around," he'd told her. "You're not a puppet on a string." They'd lost touch but she'd always remember him. She covered her anger with a cool smile. "I've got a *new* `beau' as it happens."

"Ah." They exchanged looks. She could almost hear the sighs of relief.

"You can certainly do better than *Steven*," her mother said with a sniff. "What with that earring stuck in his ear, and a degree in *Sociology*!"

Her father looked thoughtful. "Who's this one then, Ruth? Decent background, I hope, not like that last chap? In your year, was he?"

"One thing at a time, Dad." God, they were such snobs. She sat back in her chair "To start with, he wasn't taking a degree at all. He wasn't even at University."

They stared at her. Her father gulped down some tea, almost burning his throat in the process. He wiped his mouth, carefully. "Older than you, I expect. In his father's business perhaps?"

"Hardly. I doubt if Sam even knows who his father *is*. He had a deprived childhood."

"Oh dear, I don't think I want to hear any more. Most unfortunate." Her mother got up with a frown and began to fuss around with the tea-tray, brushing up crumbs, checking the milk jug. "More tea anyone?"

Ruth's father drained his cup and held it out. He turned to Ruth. "What work does he do then, Ruth? A tough childhood needn't be a handicap. I've known plenty rise above it."

Ruth braced herself. They weren't going to like this. "Officially, he's unemployed and on social security. It's hard getting work, if you're unskilled."

"Unskilled? Oh, God!" Her father almost spilt his tea into his saucer. He recovered his composure with a tight smile. "Ah, well, at your age, boyfriends come and go. It's seldom serious. Having a good degree *is*. So how did you do?"

"Did you get a First?" her mother asked. "You've done so well up to now, darling. They're really impressed at the Country Club with all those alphas you got in your first year."

Their eyes probed her. Ruth swallowed the last of her tea. She suddenly felt like a fly caught in a web. She moved to the French Windows, aware of their eyes following her as she peered out. "The garden's a tip," she remarked in an off-hand tone. "Fred losing his touch?"

Her father said, shortly, "We don't have Fred any more. He's given up because of his arthritis. And it's a devil of a job finding someone else."

"Hm. The upper branches of that cedar could do with lopping. And the rock garden's a mess…"

"Forget the garden!" Her father slapped his hand down on the coffee-table. "Why are you changing the subject, Ruth? If you didn't get a First, then say so." He shrugged. "A two-one is perfectly acceptable. We can cope with that. Right, Jess?" He turned to his wife.

Ruth glanced from one to the other. Cope with it? They'd be choked. Her mother had probably bragged to everyone already that her daughter's First was a cinch.

She sat down again, hands clasping her knees. "A lot has happened since I last saw you."

"I dare say," her father snapped. "But could we focus on your *results* for the moment? You're not going to let us down, I hope. Not after having done so well." He added, quietly, "and after the expense we've gone to."

Ruth winced. She'd pay them back. Every penny.

They waited.

She crumbled a piece of scone in her fingers. "I'd sooner tell you my other news first." She paused. "To start with, my boy-friend, Sam, is Afro-Caribbean."

Silence. Her words had taken their breath away.

Ruth watched them, a twinge of unease starting up in her chest. Her mother was fidgeting with her pearls, and flicking an imaginary crumb from her paisley blouse. Her father was drumming his fingers on the arms of his chair, something he often did when trying to digest something unpleasant

"I see," he said at last. He folded his arms. "Are you sure that's - er -wise? Not that we're racist. Far from it. Nothing wrong with the professional, well educated sort. But a fellow with no qualifications, no job …. Hardly a catch, you must admit."

"We couldn't possibly invite him to the country club," her mother said. She smiled, but Ruth could see that the smile was forced and over-bright, and she knew from the iciness of her tone and the stiff set of her shoulders that her mother was far from pleased.

Soon, however, she seemed to shuffle off her displeasure and, turning to Ruth, said, eagerly, "By the way, darling, we often meet Ralph there, and that young doctor, James Chandos-Pole. They're always asking about you. Wouldn't you like to meet them again? They're much more *us*."

Ruth rolled her eyes. Meet those turkey-cocks again? She'd sooner jump off a cliff.

"Sam's more *me*," she told them with a defiant tilt of her chin. "The only trouble is …" She halted and took a deep breath. "He's into drugs."

Her mother's eyebrows almost vanished under her blonde fringe. "You mean Cannabis?"

Ruth gave a brittle laugh. "The harder stuff, I'm afraid."

"What?" Both parents jumped up at once.

"Are you serious?" Her father's anger ripped the air. "What the hell are you doing, getting involved with a man like that? For God's sake, dump him. Before I do it for you."

"It's too late now. You see, he's got *me* hooked too. And there's something else." Ruth stopped and took another deep breath. "I'm having his baby."

They gasped. Her mother, sinking into her chair again, flung up her hands. "Heaven help us!"

Her father marched over to Ruth and seized her by the shoulders. "Where does this fellow live?" His eyes were pools of fury now. "If he's into drugs, we'll get the police to sort him out."

Ruth steadied her voice. "Don't worry, Dad. We're going to do the right thing. We're getting *married*. Once Sam's got enough money, he's moving back to Jamaica and taking me with him."

She studied their faces, the open mouths, staring eyes. Guilt began to gnaw at her. She ignored it and went on, doggedly, "If I help him with his next job, that should see us through."

"Next job? What's that? Transporting drugs? Like hell you will."

Ruth watched her father pace up and down the room like a caged beast, hands pushing through his mottled-grey hair, anxiety showing in every feature. She flinched. It was cruel to go on, but she had the strange feeling she was riding a roller-coaster that wouldn't stop.

Her voice came out in a rasp. "Well, it's either that or going back on the *game*. We've got to get the money together somehow."

"On the game? You mean *selling* yourself?" He spun round to face her, then stood, shaking his head in bewilderment. "I don't believe this."

Her mother tottered to her feet, face the colour of chalk. She gasped out, "Oh, Ruth, how could you?" took a tentative step towards her, swayed, and clutched at her throat.

Her husband leapt forward to give her support. "See what you've done?" he flung back at Ruth. "You know the state of your mother's health."

He helped settle her on the chair again, rubbing her hands and murmuring, "It's all right, Jess. I'm here."

Ruth gazed at her parents in anguish, the remains of scone in her mouth tasting bitter now. She'd gone too far. Her father was shaking and biting his lip, while her mother sat, crumpled on the chair, tears trickling down her face.

"By the way," she faltered, "I failed my finals."

They gaped at her, as if not understanding. At last, her father burst out, "You think we *care*? Now? After this?" He clenched his hands. "You're pregnant, marrying a drug-dealer, on the game. And you think we give a toss about your exams?"

Ruth set her cup and saucer on the table and got up. "I'm glad you feel that way," she said, her voice trembling, "because it's the only piece of news I've given you that's *true*."

They looked at her, blankly. Then, as her words sank in, she saw the shock on their faces slowly give way to relief.

But two red spots of anger remained on her father's cheeks, and grew brighter. "You mean that everything you've told us is a pack of lies? Some sort of joke?" His voice was dangerously quiet. "Your mother almost collapsed, damn it."

Her mother wiped tears from her eyes. "Why, Ruth, why? How could you be so cruel?"

Ruth stepped over and kissed her. "Sorry, Mother." She turned to her father. "Sorry, Dad."

She sat down. "I was just trying to show you how I *might* have failed. I could have got hooked on drugs, married a criminal, become a prostitute. But all I did was *fail an exam*. I wanted you to see it in perspective."

There was silence a moment. Finally, her father unclenched his hands and slumped into his chair. "Okay. Point taken." He sighed. "I thought you were a high flyer, that's all. I thought you *wanted* to read Economics."

"No, Dad. *You* wanted me to read Economics. I worked my guts out in my first year to get those *A*s just to please you. But when I reached my final year, I got utterly lost and gave up. So I took a course in landscape gardening, something I've always wanted to do. And it suits me fine. I'm not like you. I'm the practical type. And I'm sick of being moulded into something I'm not. *That's* why I told you all those lies."

She stepped towards the French Windows and glanced out. "Why don't I design a really nice garden for you in the spring? It would be a way of paying you back."

She turned to face her parents.

They looked away and said nothing for a while. At last her father rose and stepped towards her.

He laid an awkward hand on her shoulder and squeezed it. "Why don't you do that?" he murmured.

WAITING FOR POLLY

This story is based on a true event that occurred in 1992

The call came when I was in the kitchen, fixing dinner.

With a groan of irritation, I snatched the receiver from its cradle and barked into it, "Yes?"

The voice that answered was young, hesitant.

"Hullo. Is that Jane Ross? My name's Polly. Is it okay to talk?" She paused. "I'm your daughter. Could we meet some time?"

In an instant the spluttering of steak frying and the smell of onions faded from my consciousness. My daughter?

I sank into a chair, struggling to maintain my grip on the telephone. I could hardly breathe. Nineteen sixty-two, I thought, when I last saw her. Thirty years ago. She was a baby. Over and over again I'd tried to trace her, but the Adoption Agency refused even to give me her name. And now, at last ...

My voice came out faint, quavery, as I replied, "I'd love to, Polly."

That was the day before yesterday. Today I'm standing outside Romano's at the corner of Baker Street where we've arranged to meet for lunch. It's close to Polly's work place and not too out-of-the-way for me. My husband, Ben, knows my secret. He wanted to come too. But I decided to meet Polly alone this first time.

While I'm waiting here, fumes from a noisy stream of traffic assault my nose and mingle with the smell of coffee drifting out of Romano's each time the door opens and shuts.

My heart is racing as I scan each young woman who passes by, wondering if it can be this one or that one. Now summer's over, they're mostly dressed in browns or blacks. I don't know what Polly will be wearing. `Small and slim' is all I have by way of description.

Anyway, she's bound to see me standing here. I've told her what I look like and how I'll be dressed. Once she glimpses my fuzz of greying hair and navy trouser-suit she'll guess it's me. We'll exchange smiles, and go for a bite to eat. It will be lovely.

At least, I hope so.

Her call had sent me tingling with excitement. At last I would meet again my one and only child. But now I'm having qualms. How will we get on? Will she like me? Will I like her?

The questions running through my head make my pulse race, my palms feel clammy. She'll quiz me perhaps. Demand answers to awkward questions. And how should I respond? Honesty is the best policy, they say. But sometimes the truth can be too brutal. I'll play it by ear.

A passer-by in a maroon skirt and jacket stops and gives me a quick glance up and down. Is it *her*? She's slim and about my height, with dark hair, cascading down her back. And her eyes are blue, like mine, though bigger and brighter. She gives me a tentative smile.

It *is* her. My heart starts to beat very fast.

"Hullo, you must be Jane. Great to meet you." She holds out her hand.

We go into Romano's and grab a table for two in a corner.

I can't stop staring at her. She's quite good-looking with her olive skin, and dark, curling eye-lashes. Not that looks matter. Just the same, I'm glad she's attractive.

"I often come here in the lunch break," she says. Her tone is soft, lilting.

I'm suddenly at a loss for words, and I can feel my face getting hot. I put on my busy, taking-charge voice. "What will you have, Polly?"

"Just an orange juice, please, and some salad. I'm vegetarian."

"Is that on principle? Or for health reasons?"

She shrugs. "On principle, I suppose. I hate the thought of things being killed for us to eat."

"That's just how I feel." I look up from my menu in surprise. "I couldn't become vegetarian, though. If I did, I'd probably starve. I *hate* vegetables." I give a self-conscious laugh before plying her with anecdotes about my beloved cats, Mimi and Lulu.

Oh dear. I pause. I'm beginning to gabble. How embarrassing! And I so much wanted to make a good impression.

The waitress comes to take our order.

When she goes, I'm tongue-tied again.

Polly helps me out. "Perhaps you'd like to know something about *me*?"

I nod, glad to let her take the reins. She seems anxious to put me at ease. It's nice of her. I wish though it was *I* trying to put *her* at ease. I'm the mother after all.

She tells me about her home in Surrey with her adoptive parents, her plan to move into a flat soon. "Not that I'm unhappy at home," she assures me. "The family's great. But I *am* pushing thirty. It's about time I moved out."

She talks eagerly about her work. "I took art at university," she tells me, "Since then, I've been with a publishing firm, illustrating children's books."

She got that from me perhaps. *I* was good at art once.

She turns to the subject of her boy-friend and her eyes begin to sparkle. "John's an insurance broker," she says. "He came with me to the Adoption Agency for information, and helped me trace you. He's clever at things like that."

She's done well, I must say. Good education, clever boy-friend, work she enjoys. How well would she have done, I wonder, with a lone mother struggling to bring her up?

I can't take my eyes off her. It sounds barmy, I know, but the idea that I'd actually produced another human being who could walk, talk, paint pictures and be a vegetarian struck me as amazing.

She looks anxious a moment. "I hope it's not a problem, meeting me like this? I'm not needing help or anything. It's just that …" She pauses, searching for words. "I've had this urge to find my birth parents, discover my roots. I kept dreaming about it."

Then comes the dreaded question, "Didn't you *want* to have me?"

She's frowning now, leaning forward, her eyes flickering over my face. I feel my cheeks beginning to burn again.

No, I didn't want to have you, the voice in my head answers. If abortions had been legal at that time, I'd have gone for one like a shot. As it was, I did my best to drown you with gin, poison you with obnoxious powders and blast you to smithereens through deliberate tumbles down stairs. Nothing worked. I was stuck with you.

I clear my throat and reply, "I didn't, at first." I toy with my napkin. "Soon after you were born, though, I was desperate to *keep* you. But I had no means. I lived alone, you see. It was difficult for single mothers in those days."

She smooths back her hair, breaks into a smile. "Of course. I understand. And there was the stigma too back then, wasn't there?"

I nod, recalling the raised eyebrows and frowns of disapproval. Although it was 1962, it wasn't yet the 'swinging sixties'. Waves of half-forgotten shame flow in again, like the returning tide. I'll lose my teaching job, I wailed, once they find out. How will I cope? Run to my parents for help? No way. They had worries of their own. Seek *him*, the father? I'd die first. In mounting panic, I pretended I'd got married. I dumped my real name, Miss Harris, and became Mrs Barclay instead. Six months passed before the education authority caught on and called me for an interview. It made me squirm, having finally to blurt out the truth.

Then came the horror of putting myself in the hands of social services, and moving to a mother-and-baby home. And, finally, the hospital stay, when the baby was due. I was the only one on the ward with no husband to visit her. The snide whispers of other mothers didn't help. Nor did the yelling out of my true title, *Miss* Harris, by a spiteful nurse.

The waitress bustles up with the omelette I've ordered, and my daughter's salad.

Polly adjusts her napkin. "And what about my father? Do you know where he is?

My mouthful of omelette acquires a sour taste. Here comes the creative part. I haven't yet made up my mind what to say about *him*. "He's dead," I mumble at last. I look away. Well, perhaps he is by this time.

"Oh dear." A frown puckers her forehead. She looks disappointed. "Dead?"

"Well, not exactly." I shift in my chair. It's no use going along that route. One lie will only lead to another. "He's just dead to *me*, that's all." My voice sounds thin, like paper rustling. "And I don't know where he is.

It happened at a party, you see. There was too much to drink and …" I shrug.

She can see I'm embarrassed. She smiles, gently. "It's all right. Stuff happens." She picks at her lettuce. "I've found you anyway. That's the main thing."

I smile back at her, relieved. She's making things so easy. I've told her she's the end-product of a one-night stand. And she takes it in her stride.

What if I'd told her the *truth*, though, the whole truth?

What if I told her I'd stupidly gone out with a man, not because I liked him but because his constant pestering wore me down. My date with him for lunch was meant to be just *that*: lunch. But as we left the restaurant, it began to rain. "My pad's just down the road," he said. "It's a lot nearer than the tube station. Why not shelter there till the rain stops?"

I hesitated. "I'd sooner go straight home."

"And get soaked? What's the matter? Do you think I'm going to rape you or something?"

"Of course not."

I followed him in. He poured me a drink, then another and another. I began to feel hazy. I'm not used to drink and I shouldn't have let him press me into having more than one. I got up, unsteady on my feet. "Must go. It's stopped raining. Thanks for the lunch."

I staggered to the door.

He'd locked it.

I turned, my head spinning. That's when he grabbed me and clapped his hands over my mouth.

I couldn't have told her all that. Any more than I could have told how I'd tried to abort her. Or how I wouldn't even *look* at her for two whole days after she was born, that, initially, I had rejected her. There are some truths that are better left unsaid.

She finishes her salad. "At least, you didn't get an abortion. I'm dead against abortions."

I wince. I can see she feels strongly about this. She's tossing back her hair, and her eyes are flashing. She's not as passive as I thought.

"I did want to keep you," I say, trying to steady my voice. "Not straight away, but once we got … attached. I even tried to get you back after you'd been adopted. But it was too late. And it wouldn't have been fair to you or your adoptive parents."

She nods her agreement.

I feel happier now. The hard part is over. I finish my omelette and order a lemon mousse for Polly and an ice cream for me.

We chat about other things, about my husband, Ben, our village in Hertfordshire, and my all-consuming hobby: amateur dramatics. "I used to be professional once," I tell her.

Our talk becomes more animated. "I love acting too," she says. "John and I belong to the local drama society. We'll soon start rehearsing for the Christmas pantomime, *Aladdin.* Perhaps you and Ben would like to come?" She pauses, eye-brows raised in question. "He does know about me?"

"Of course," I say. "And he's dying to meet you."

We seem to have much in common. Maybe there's more to heredity than meets the eye.

Anyway, our meeting goes with a swing after that. Our mutual love of the theatre has broken the ice.

We shall meet again, I know. My inhibitions have gone. So have my regrets. It hadn't been easy, being unmarried and pregnant in those days. But I'm glad now I failed to have that abortion. I'd had a child, a living, feeling human being. The thought makes my inside glow with pleasure.

"Let's meet again. Soon," I say.

She takes out her diary.

TALKING TO MAGGIE

Well, here I am, Maggie, my love, relaxing outside the shops in Langley Square. Not *my* idea, mind you – you know what *I* think of shopping. No, it's Jo's, bless her, wanting to get the roses back in my cheeks.

"You need more fresh air, Dad," she says. So every Thursday, on her day off, over she trots, ready to strap me into *Fiona* – that's my new wheelchair - and hustle me out.

I can put up with the fresh air bit. But shopping? I enjoy shopping like I enjoy a cold in the head.

The worst thing about it is being trundled through this cobbled square. It gives a chap's innards no end of a shaking, to say nothing of a sore backside. That part of me hasn't got the flesh on it that it used to have. But I can't tell our daughter that. You know how she goes off the deep end.

She's popped into the off-licence to get a bottle of Scotch. Oh, don't worry, Maggie, love, it's not for me. It's for Chris down the road. He fixed my boiler the other day and wouldn't take any money for the job. I owe him one.

I wanted to go in and choose it myself but Jo said, "You've had that, dad. There's no ramp, and I can't heave you up over that step."

She's got a point. She's a hefty lass, but not *that* hefty.

"Fair enough," I said. "Leave me by the entrance then. I'll ruminate."

She put on the brake and gave me a quick glance.

"Sure you wouldn't like me to get *you* something too. A couple of drinks might cheer you up."

"Forget it," I growled.

Just the same, I can almost taste that whisky on my tongue and feel its warmth tantalizing my throat. I press my lips together, *hard*. I made a vow, and I'm sticking to it. I hope you're listening, Maggie?

It's nice to have a break from being wheeled about. Not that I should grumble. *Fiona's* much more comfortable than *Daisy*, my old wheelchair. It's nice soft leather, not that canvas stuff. *That* got my insides rattling about like pills in a bottle once we were on the move. And this new foam cushion I sent away for is a great help. It absorbs a lot of the bumps.

I look around me. Guess what, Maggie? There's a cocker-spaniel tied to a post the other side of the off-licence. He's sitting there, quiet as a lamb, gazing at me with solemn brown eyes. I smile at him. "Hullo, old fellow. We're in the same boat, you and me. Fixed to one damn spot. It's a flaming bore, isn't it?

I watch him put his head on one side while he makes a sound between a whine and a grunt. Can you see him, Maggie? He's the image of our old Patch. God, I miss having a dog around. But dogs need walks. And unless I tie his lead to my wheelchair, and let him trot beside me to the park every morning, then a dog's definitely *out*.

I watch people passing. Two girls in low-cut jeans are giving their belly-buttons an airing. In my young days I'd have treated them to a wolf whistle, but chaps don't do that any more, especially old ones in wheelchairs.

The girls are so busy chatting that one of them bumps into my chair. "Ow ... sorry," she says, hardly turning her head, and on she goes, still prattling away. Was she saying 'sorry' to *me*, I wonder, or to the wheelchair?

Others pass by. A stout woman with a face like suet-pudding gives me a quick glance and looks away again, as if embarrassed at the sight. Can't think why. There are plenty of us around. Then an old biddy with a shopping-trolley nearly as big as herself treats me to a nod and a hint of a smile, as if to acknowledge my existence.

I don't like to grouse, but I can think of more exciting things to do than sitting here gawping at people. Remember our adventure holidays, Maggie? Our trips to North Africa and the Greek islands? The time you tried water-skiing but your skis were too big and kept slipping off? Our goes at snorkelling?

None of that now. Travel's become a no-no. Jo and Pete have offered to take me to Spain, but there's too much hassle. The questions you have to ask before going anywhere! Are there lifts? Will there be a ramp? Are doors wide enough to let wheelchairs through? Etcetera, etcetera. And you'd need to be tough as an old boot to go away on your own.

Still, mustn't grumble. Things could be worse. At least my arms are okay. In fact, they've grown quite muscly over the years. Just as well, considering the way I have to heave myself out of the chair and into bed at night, or onto the loo. I can still dress myself, and, with the help of old *Fiona* here, I can wheel myself into the kitchen and make a cup of tea and toast, or stick ready-meals in the oven … Thank God for ready-meals!

You're done for, though, without a sense of humour, especially when you're with people who treat wheelchair users as if they're invisible or from another planet. Sometimes they'll ask your attendant questions like, "Has he eaten?" and "What time does he have lunch?" while you're right there in the room with them.

It's irritating but I keep my cool. And, before my attendant has a chance to reply, I butt in with a smile, "No, *he* hasn't eaten, and *he* usually has lunch between twelve and one." For God's sake! Do they think we're dumb as well as crippled?

A sense of humour came in handy the other day. If you're listening, Maggie, this will make you laugh: I was round the corner, in my wheelchair, minding my own business, when a little kid, passing by, nudged her mother and said, "Mummy, why is that man in a pram?"

Her mother said, "Ssh!" and pulled her away.

It creased me up. Pram indeed! But in a way she's right. I'm a man in a pram, wheeled around like a baby. And why? Well, *we* know why, don't we, Maggie?

A joyful barking starts up. A lanky youth steps out of Hammets next door and unties the cocker-spaniel.

"Nice dog," I say. "I used to have one like that."

He gives me a wide smile. "Yes, he's great. Don't know what I'd do without him." He steps towards me. "You can stroke him, if you like. He's ever so friendly."

It's given me quite a lift stroking that dog, Maggie. Remember how we used to stroke Patch, how we'd laugh at the fuss he'd make when it was time for his walk, how we'd scold him for the tricks he got up to, like chasing the cat next door?

Our Jo's coming out of the shop at last, a plastic bag clutched in her hand. "I got your Scotch, dad. Single Malt, like you asked."

She puts the bag on my lap. It's heavy, and there's a sound of bottles clinking.

I frown. "What else you got in there?"

"Just a bottle of red wine. Thought we'd have a glass this evening before I go. It shouldn't do you any harm. They say it's good for the heart."

I tighten my lips. "They can say what they like, but you count me out. Keep it for you and Pete."

She means well, our Jo, but she doesn't understand the half of it. She knows about the *accident*, of course. But *why* it happened is another story. And I'm sorry, Maggie, but I haven't got round to telling her about that.

I've missed you, love, and our life together. The house feels so empty now. It's not that I don't get company. Carers come in from time to time, as well as the district nurse and the home-help. And there's our daughter of course. She doesn't forget her old dad. She'd have me move in with her and Pete, if I wasn't so independent.

They're all a godsend, but they're not *you*.

You warned me about my drinking, remember? But all I did was bite your head off.

"You're over the limit, Frank," you said that night. "Let *me* drive."

I pushed you away. "Quit nagging woman, I'm fine."

I plonked myself in the driving-seat, puffed up with tipsy, couldn't-give-a-hang defiance. And then ... well, you know the rest: the skidding, the screeching of brakes, that final spine-shattering blast-from-hell, which left me in this wheelchair and you, *dead*.

Seven years have passed since then, and I'm still thinking about you, Maggie, and the love we had between us. I'm not a religious man, but I can't help hoping that you're up there somewhere, ready to forgive, and to say:

"I've been waiting for you, Frank, love. Never mind the past. You've done your penance. Now give me a hug."

THE LAST GOODBYE

I can hear Aunt Pru's howl of protest directly I step into the porch of Arcadia Hall.

"Legal, you say?" she squawks. "Clare's legal choice? We'll see about that."

Oh dear. She's not going to make a scene I hope? I've had enough of scenes for one morning, coping with those protesters outside, waving their banners at me.

Pulling off my face-mask, I drop it in the recycling-bin at the corner of the porch - air pollution seems thicker than usual this morning. Then, I poke my head through the part-open door of the hall and glance inside.

As expected: Hordes of people milling about, chatting, sipping wine, all eager to see Aunt Clare for the last time. Real, fresh flowers displayed on stands, the scents of lilies and honeysuckle mingling with the smells of cocktail- savouries laid out on a trestle-table at the far side: the feast to follow the last goodbyes. And not a bad one, in view of today's rationing.

A ceremonial-attendant in the customary mauve dress with white collar is at the wine-table pouring wine into glasses. Another is arranging chairs in rows facing a platform at the front of the hall. On it stands an elaborate gilt chair, like a throne, with three ordinary chairs on either side.

I feel a shiver run through me. Soon, my aunt will be sitting up there, facing us, ready to say goodbye. The prospect unsettles me. Taking deep breaths to calm myself, I step inside, wending my way through the huddles of guests, mumbling "Excuse me" or "So sorry," as I brush past.

They're mostly strangers to me, probably friends and admirers of my aunt. She's done much charity work over the years, on top of being a devoted wife and mother.

Among the guests, I catch sight of Cousin David, Clare's son. His hair is streaked with grey now, as is his beard. He looks the typical professor. His sister, Jane is beside him, dabbing at her eyes with a handkerchief while, nearby, Aunt Pru, a simmering cauldron of disapproval, stands out from the crowd in her black dress. Dark colours are no longer fashionable at these events, but Pru has always clung to tradition.

Ah, Jane has spotted me. She scurries up and gives me a hug. I feel my eyes fill with tears and my shoulders begin to shake. "Don't cry, Kate," she says, her own eyes glistening. "Mother has made her choice, and it's not for us to interfere." She smiles and pats my cheek. "We must try to be cheerful on her last day, not shed tears when we say goodbye."

I don't know why I'm crying. If I'm honest, I feel little warmth towards Aunt Clare. I admire her, of course. She's a saint. But I'm uncomfortable with saints. I fancy they can see into my soul and examine the sins there. I'm not looking forward to that last goodbye, that last hug. I shall feel so awkward.

Jane studies my face, her eyes troubled. "Did they bother you, those protesters outside?"

"Not too much. The police have them under control." I pause and bite my lip. "They're dead against this new law."

"And you? Are you against it?"

I shrug. "I'm not sure yet. It goes much further than the 2062 Act. A step too far perhaps."

"Not far enough according to Mother. In a crisis like this, she says, we should follow the Dutch or Chinese example. Anyway, she's determined to go ahead." I hear a quiver in her voice. "It's a bit hard on those who love her. Still, we mustn't …" She breaks off and gives me a nudge. "Watch out. Here comes trouble."

Turning, I see Aunt Pru, elbowing her way towards us. In that black dress, she puts me in mind of the bad fairy at a christening.

"This is never Clare's choice," she rasps. "Someone's pulling her strings, you mark my words." She gives a grunt. "Duty to the State indeed! Concern for the planet! It's that precious son of hers, putting ideas in her head."

She gestures towards a spot near the trestle-table where David is talking animatedly to a group of guests. "Look at him. See how he's got them all nodding and hanging on to his every word?" She rolls her eyes. "And you can guess what he's ranting about. Same old gloom and doom: how our planet is overcrowded, choking from pollution, how resources are dwindling. Ugh! He's such a bore."

Jane clicks her tongue. "Get your head out of the sand, Aunt Pru. Why do you think we've started rationing - food, fuel, even medical supplies? Why the need for face-masks? We have a population crisis. The birth rate's been going down in some countries but not fast enough. In others it's been going up. There's not even enough good air to go round."

"Balderdash! What's needed is more research. Better planning of resources."

"We've left it too late, I'm afraid. As David says, only drastic measures will save us now."

Pru gives a snort. "*David says, David says*. I see he's got you in his grip, as well as his mother."

Jane reddens. "Stop bitching about David, Aunt Pru. Mother has a mind of her own. She's made her choice and that's that. It's a legal option."

Pru tightens her hands into fists. "And it's wrong. It's the slippery slope. First, there's the Option for the chronically sick and disabled. Now this: Option for the over-eighty-fives, sick or not. What's next, I wonder?"

I shake my head. That slippery slope stuff is so twentieth century. Even so, this new law, giving the option to all old people - I'm still not sure about that.

I glance at my watch. Ten o'clock. The ceremonial-attendants have finished arranging the chairs. People are putting down their drinks and finding seats. Soon the *exiteers*, nurses and witnesses file in and seat themselves on either side of the Ceremonial Chair.

Then comes the Speech-Maker, a portly man with shiny, bald head and a habit of clasping and un-clasping his hands. "Good morning, friends. Please sit." He raises his arms as if to conduct an orchestra. Those still lingering at the tables hurry to find seats.

The Speech-Maker coughs and begins, "We are gathered here today to celebrate the life of Mrs Clare Hawkins and to say our goodbyes on her last day." He pauses.

The side-door opens and in walks Clare, her dressers on either side. She is wearing the regular white robe which reaches to her feet, with matching cloak on top. Later, I know, the cloak will be removed and one of the nurses will take her arm, while an *exiteer* applies the injection. I shudder.

There are sighs of admiration as she makes her entrance. She's still a handsome woman, I reflect, even at eighty-five. Her cheeks are scarcely wrinkled, and her silver hair, piled up in waves, has a sheen that many young people would be proud of. She walks upright without need of assistance.

Tears moisten my eyes again. Why doesn't she wait? Eighty-five isn't so old. Some that age are still jogging or playing golf. Perhaps, as Jane says, she's making a statement – telling us that in these tough times, life-span should be rationed, along with food and other resources.

The Speech-Maker begins his talk about my aunt's life, her useful work in the community, the pillar of strength she'd been to her late husband, Glen.

Clare smiles, nods or shakes her head in dismissal.

Then David steps up to the platform to make his speech. "My mother's departure will be a great loss to us," he begins in his rich baritone, "but no begging or pleading would persuade her to stay longer."

He pauses to steady the sudden tremor in his voice. "You all know her views on population. `What's the point in lowering the birth rate if, at the same time, we force the old and infirm to stay alive?' she asks. `All we get that way is an age imbalance, with the State unable to cope.' That's why, my friends, she's taking advantage of this new law. As a woman of principle, she insists on doing what she thinks is right."

Murmurs of approval turn to gasps of horror as Pru rises from her chair and bursts out, "Rubbish!"

Jane tries to pull her back but Pru pushes her away. "My sister's been coerced into this," she shouts.

Clare stumbles to her feet. The ceremonial-attendants, *exiteers* and witnesses exchange glances, undecided what to do.

At last the Speech-Maker steps forward and holds up his hand. "Peace, lady. All such suspicions should have been brought to the Panel before the Ceremony. This is most irregular."

Pru looks him straight in the eye. "If there's any evidence of coercion, the ceremony can be stopped even now. I know the law."

Clare finds her voice at last. It rings out firm, distinct. "Let's have your evidence, Pru. I'm curious to know who coerced me."

"I have it right here." Pru clicks open her handbag, pulls out a fax, and waves it in front of her. "I found this in one of your files, Clare. Shall I read it out?" Meeting her sister's angry stare, she pauses. "Okay, I snooped. And just as well. She glances around her, a look of defiance on her face. Everyone bends forward, eager-eyed, waiting.

Adjusting her glasses, Pru begins to read, `Take my advice, Mother, and end things. You know it's the right thing to do – David'.

There are more gasps as everyone stares at David still standing at his mother's side.

I chew my lip. Oh dear. He's in trouble, if it's proved he coerced his mother.

The Speech-Maker frowns. "This is a serious allegation."

"It's *coercion*." Pru wags a finger at David. "That man is no better than a murderer. He can't wait to get at his mother's money so he can finance his campaigns and get rid of the rest of us old folk."

There is a chorus of shocked muttering which soon develops into a noisy free-for-all, with people arguing, shouting and twisting in their seats. Some, siding with Pru, are yelling, "Listen to her, Clare" and "Don't be pressurised. You're not ready for the scrapheap yet." But just as vocal are the cries of "Slander!" and "Throw her out!" aimed at Pru.

A worried looking Speech-Maker calls for order. The noise dies down.

David, silent, wipes a bead of sweat from his forehead. Finally, recovering his composure, he says in steady tones, "That fax was written at least ten years ago. It's private – nothing to do with this matter at all."

The Speech-Maker shuffles his feet and sighs. "Perhaps we'd better postpone the Ceremony until things are sorted out."

"No." Clare sinks back into her seat and falters, "I can explain. David was advising me to end a relationship, not my life."

"Leave it, Mother. It's not necessary,"

"Yes, it is. I won't have you suffer for my mistakes. She squares her shoulders and looks straight in front of her. "My relationship was with someone who gave me comfort when my husband was terminally ill. It was wrong, and I ended it. I hope that satisfies you, Pru."

Pru gapes at her sister. So do I. Until three years ago, my aunt's husband was still alive. Yet there she was, having a relationship with someone else. I could scarcely believe it. Aunt Clare, the perfect wife, pillar of loyalty to my Uncle Glen? A feeling of warmth towards her sweeps over me. So my aunt had flaws. She was a human being like the rest of us.

A hush follows this revelation. It's broken by a woman in the back row who calls out, "Whatever Clare's mistake, she's still a fine person in my book."

"Hear, hear!" someone else cries. "Brave too." He starts to clap. Soon everyone is clapping, and there are calls of 'Speech'.

Clare gestures for it to stop. "Brave? Absolutely not. I'm a tired old crumbly in declining health. Why wait till I sink into dotage when I can go *now*, with some dignity and independence, privileges I certainly won't get at our overcrowded hospitals or care homes.

She gives a grim smile. "We're living longer, I know, but medical progress has its limitations. We still can't escape disease and disability in our later years, or our need of support." She heaves a sigh. "The pity is that the old and the terminally ill have had to wait for a population crisis before their cries for release were listened to."

Her eyes flicker over her audience, resting at last on her sister. "No one's infringed my human rights. The choice is mine. I've had a good life, and good friends. I want to *see* them before I go."

The Speech-Maker, consulting his watch again, calls for silence. "I think it's time for the filing past so you can say your goodbyes to Clare."

One by one, starting with the first row, we step onto the platform to pause at my aunt's chair and bid her goodbye. There are many people so we must be brief.

Each takes her hand and kisses her cheek. I hug her close, my awkwardness gone. "We'll miss you, Aunt Clare," I say. I mean it. Her face lights up. "My dear girl, I didn't think you cared," she murmurs.

When all goodbyes are said, Clare rises and, with her ceremonial-attendants, glides towards the side-door, behind the *exiteers* and witnesses. The moans and sighs that follow are drowned by a recording of Bach's *Air on the G-string* starting up.

At the door Clare turns briefly to face us and smiles.

This, I reflect, is how people will remember her, a woman of spirit in her white robe, not a crumpled remnant of decaying humanity, bound to her bed. I've finally made up my mind. If I'm still around at eighty-five and finished my life's work, I'll not wait, after all. I'll take the same option, death with dignity and with friends around me. Why wait till they cease to come?

There is a shuffling of chairs and people are rising and making their way to the back of the hall. I shake off my musings and return to practicalities. It's time to eat. The attendants are at the buffet-table, handing out plates and pouring wine.

I follow the others and wait my turn.

TIME TO SMILE

This section contains a miscellany of light-hearted stories, some set in current times, others, such as *Dejeuner sur L'herbe,* set in the past. Set even further in the past is the tale *Plum Pudding* which, even though a fairy tale, will, hopefully, amuse.
The last five stories narrate incidents in my own life with my late husband, Patrick.

A BOX OF CHALKS

Henry could hear her, from the bathroom, giving Robert one of her `heart to hearts'.

"Now you *will* be a good boy, won't you, darling? You won't bounce like this over Uncle Edward's furniture or finger his valuable ornaments? You will *behave*?"

Henry flung down his hair-brush and hurried to the sitting-room. He stopped with a jerk at the doorway as he saw his son doing what looked like a parachute-jump off the sofa and taking not a blind bit of notice of his mother's begging and pleading.

"Now don't forget, sweetheart," she was saying, her voice like melted toffee, "it's important we keep on good terms with Uncle Edward, so just be a nice, polite boy, and remember to say `thank you' if he offers you a bun or anything ... Are you listening, Robert?"

Henry threw up his hands. God Almighty, of course he wasn't listening! The kid was hyperactive. He should be on Ritalin. He strode into the room. "Hell, Vicky, can't you stop that child? We won't have a home left by the time he's finished with it."

Robert was about to make one last jump when his father grabbed him by the shoulders and sat him down on the sofa. "Now just you listen to me, Batman," he said, jabbing a finger at him, "we don't want any problems at Uncle Edward's, okay? There's to be no yelling or racing about, no personal remarks and no face-pulling behind your uncle's back. Got it?"

He pulled him up. "Now, quick march to the bathroom! We're already late."

Robert saluted stiffly. Then, with a solemn goose-step picked up from an old World-War 11 film, he made his way to the bathroom.

"If Uncle Edward does die soon and leave us all his money, the first thing I shall do is send that child to boarding-school," Henry muttered.

After a drive of nearly two hours, Henry brought the car to a halt outside Uncle Edward's elegant Georgian house. Mrs Banks, the housekeeper, all plump smiles, showed them into the drawing room where Uncle Edward tottered to his feet to greet them.

"Well, well, how nice of you to come all this way to see an old wrinkly like me," he wheezed.

"Not at all, Uncle Edward. It's super to see you. And how marvellous you look! One would never take you for eighty, would one, Henry?"

"Indeed not," Henry lied, dutifully. He popped a carrier-bag onto the marble coffee-table. "I've brought your favourite brandy," he said, "and Vicky's got you some chocolate gingers."

Uncle Edward gave a bow. "How kind!"

Henry watched him turn his gaze to Robert. "My goodness, you *have* grown!"

"Yes, hasn't he? He's nine now," Vicky said, while Henry hissed in his ear, "Say 'hullo' to Uncle."

"Hullo, Uncle Edward. Nice to see you," Robert chanted, moving nearer the coffee-table and eyeing the chocolate gingers. Henry pulled him away, smartly.

"What a polite little boy!" the old man exclaimed, "Not like most youngsters of today. And that reminds me …" He smiled at Robert, his eyes twinkling. "I've got a little project I'd like you to tackle while we grown-ups are busy chatting."

He turned and walked his slow, shuffling walk to the mahogany corner-cupboard. Robert watched him, a look of deep concentration on his face, as if, Henry thought, with a twinge of unease, he were mentally rehearsing it, in the hope of trying it out later.

"Here we are, son." With a shaky hand, the old man passed Robert a bulky packet.

Robert opened it and drew out a child's colouring-book and a box of coloured chalks. He wrinkled up his nose in disgust.

Henry threw him a warning look. "What do you say to Uncle Edward?"

"Thank you, Uncle Edward," Robert mumbled.

The old man's face crinkled into a smile. "Now let's see how many pictures you can colour by the end of the afternoon. Tell you what, I'll give you fifty pence for every picture you finish. I want good work though, mind."

Disgust rapidly gave way to joy as Robert counted the pictures in the book. There were twenty.

He settled himself in a corner of the room, a determined frown on his face.

His parents breathed sighs of relief. What a wonderful idea for keeping Robert quiet! They turned to Uncle Edward who began chatting about his recent improvements to the house.

"There's a brand new kitchen now and an extra bathroom," he said. "Oh, and I've bought one or two fine pieces of silver I must show you, and some new pictures. Have you noticed the one above the fireplace?"

They looked.

"I believe I've seen it before," Henry said, puckering up his forehead and wishing he'd done more homework on art before their visit.

"Of course, darling. It's very well-known," Vicky flashed him a superior smile. "It's by Monet."

"Ah yes, how stupid of me!" He thumped his forehead.

The old man coughed. "It's by Manet, in point of fact, not Monet," he corrected them, a flicker of amusement in his eyes. "The `Dejeuner sur L'Herbe'."

Henry grunted to himself. Manet? Monet? Who cared? Reproductions weren't of any value.

Uncle Edward seemed to read his thoughts. "It's no ordinary reproduction, you know. I employed a highly skilled artist to copy the original at the Louvre." He gave a wry smile. "Made a bit of a hole in my capital, of course, but well worth it, don't you think, to have your favourite picture hanging in the drawing room?"

"Oh, I do so agree, Uncle," Vicky gushed. She stepped forward to take a closer look. "Lovely brushwork."

Henry rolled his eyes. Brushwork! What did *she* know! She was more likely trying to work out how any woman in her right mind, could possibly picnic in the nude with two men, and look so casual about it.

"It's the best reproduction I've seen." she said, turning to her uncle. "Do take us round the house to look at your other purchases. I can't wait to see them."

Henry gritted his teeth. She was no more a lover of art and antiques than he was. Still, they'd better indulge the old fellow. He forced his lips into a smile. "Lead on, Uncle."

For more than an hour they wandered from room to room, marvelling at his taste in furniture, enthusing over his antique purchases and gasping with admiration at his new pictures by up-and-coming artists.

By the end of the time, Henry could scarcely stifle his yawns, and he suspected that Vicky's `how beautiful, Uncle Edward!' and `isn't that fantastic, Henry?' must sound artificial and repetitive even to herself.

He soon gave up trying to make intelligent comments. Instead, he amused himself by totting up the likely value of Uncle Edward's Estate. He ended up with a figure of five million pounds. His heart leapt. With the old man unmarried and childless, there was a good chance Vicky would get the lot. He just hoped she wouldn't blow it all on world cruises and designer clothes. Not at least before they'd settled the mortgage and packed Robert off to boarding school … Robert? He stopped, seized by a sudden panic. "Where's Robert?"

"Don't worry, darling, he's sitting in the drawing-room, absolutely engrossed in his lovely new colouring-book."

"Well, we'd better see how the little lad is getting on," Uncle Edward said.

They made their way to the drawing-room and stopped at the doorway.

"Oh my God!" Vicky let out a gasp.

The place was a tip. Pieces of chalk lay everywhere, some bits trodden into the carpet, others smudging the coffee-table and the chaise-longue…

And there, in front of the fire-place, on a magnificent Queen Anne chair, stood Robert.

He waved his colouring-book triumphantly at Uncle Edward.

"I've finished all twenty pictures," he said, "but you'll owe me for twenty-one, Uncle, 'cause I've finished this one as well." He pointed to the 'Dejeuner'.

His parents stared at it in mounting anguish.

The picture was indeed 'finished'.

Suspended in the once empty sky was a smiling yellow sun around which hovered fantastic birds of violet and bright pink. Decorating the trees were rows of red dots representing apples. As for the nude, her transformation was complete. She was now modestly clothed from throat to ankle in what appeared to be a blue track-suit. A cigarette dangled from her mouth …

There was an awed silence, broken at last by Henry.

"You little devil. You just wait till we get home."

"Oh, Uncle Edward, your beautiful picture!"

"Please, don't worry about it." Her uncle surveyed his ruined picture with a sigh. Then he shuffled his way to the door. "I suddenly have the most appalling headache," he said, "Would you forgive me if I retire? So good of you to call. Have some tea with Mrs Banks before you go."

He went quietly out.

Robert, angry tears starting from his eyes, called after him, "What about my ten pounds fifty?" Receiving no reply, he got into his 'mad gorilla' pose and pulled his special 'killer-on-the-prowl' face, so much admired by the boys at school.

His father yanked him off the chair. "You've lost us more than ten pounds fifty," he fumed as, mentally, he waved goodbye to all hope of sending Robert to boarding-school.

They didn't stay for tea but drove straight home, Robert bawling all the way at the double disappointment of getting neither the money promised him nor the expected permission to stay up late and see 'Monster from Outer Space'. "It's not *fair*," he whined.

"Nothing's fair," Henry agreed, clenching his teeth. "There's no justice in the world."

Meanwhile, Uncle Edward, having rapidly recovered from his headache, was enjoying tea and crumpets with Mrs Banks.

"Poor Robert! He'll have his pocket money stopped, I expect, or his phone taken away," he said, shaking his head. "In my day he'd have got a walloping. Kinder in my view. Shorter lasting."

"It was rather naughty of you to tell them such a story about that picture," Mrs Banks returned, clicking her tongue, sternly. "An expensive reproduction indeed! Your cousin, Cynthia, sent you that last year, and she's so mean, I'll bet she got it from a jumble-sale for two quid."

"It's still a very nice piece of work or, rather, it *was*. Anyway ..." He gave a chuckle. "You must allow me a little fun at the expense of my awful relatives. What a tiring pair they are with their compliments and enthusiasms – and all in the hope of getting my money when I die!"

He smiled grimly into his tea. "They'll get such a disappointment when they learn that this house is left in trust to my godson, Richard, and that the rest is going to you, my dear Amelia. And you deserve it too, having to clear up all that mess in the drawing room." He pressed his housekeeper's hand, affectionately. "And now let's relax with a glass of Henry's brandy and some of those delicious chocolate gingers to round off the evening."

GETTING RID OF GLADYS

I've never forgiven my parents for calling me *Gladys*. Especially after giving my sisters romantic names like *Rosalind* and *Miranda*. I can just imagine Mum, when I came along, taking a critical look at me and saying "Hm. Something plain and solid this time, I think."

It's the way the cookie crumbles, I suppose. There I was with my wispy hair and face like the full moon, stuck with two beautiful sisters and a name like Gladys.

It was after I left school and got interested in boys that the name grew so disabling. Sometimes, I'd go clubbing with my friend, Lisa and, now and then, to my delight, some guy would try to chat me up – until he discovered my name was Gladys. At least, that's how it seemed to me. "*Gladys?*" he'd gasp, staring at me as if I'd sprouted an extra head. Then, like as not, he'd say, "I've an aunt called Gladys." And you could tell from his tone that his aunt would be plain, fat and over fifty.

At last, Lisa came up with an idea. "Why don't you get rid of Gladys?" she suggested. "I mean, if you don't like the name, why not call yourself something else?"

I looked at her blankly for a moment. But the more I thought about it, the more it seemed a great idea. Why not get rid of Gladys?

The chance came when Rosalind got married and the rest of us moved from our large house in Bromley to a smaller one in Wimbledon. No one in Wimbledon or at my new job need know about Gladys, I thought.

Even so, I probably wouldn't have taken the plunge had it not been for Miranda. Just after our move to London, she came back late one night and announced her engagement.

"Congratulations," I mumbled, half-heartedly.

Dad, sensing my left-out feeling, said, "Your turn next, Glad," while Mum chipped in with, "Maybe, if you get that job at Bentall's, you'll pick up with some nice boy there."

"I'm not looking for a boy," I snapped, feeling more of a wallflower than ever. "Some women like to be independent, you know. Have careers, run businesses and things."

Who was I kidding? I'd never make a career-woman. All I've ever wanted is to get married and have children. Pathetic isn't it? And chance would be a fine thing!

I slumped out. As I shut the door behind me, I heard Miranda say, "Poor Gladys. If only she'd do something about her hair."

That settled it. Before going to sleep that night, I decided to call myself Olivia. And the following day, I dipped into my savings, took a trip to the West End and bought a wig. A bit extreme, I know, but no hairdresser seemed able to cope with hair like mine.

And the wig was great: Coppery-gold with blonde streaks and a fringe. The assistant eased it over my head… In an instant, I changed from mouse-brown Gladys to sunset-gold Olivia. It even altered the shape of my face, making it oval instead of round.

I kept it on, and danced out of the store, tossing my shoulder-length tresses and enjoying its silky feel against my skin. I smiled at my new self through every shop-mirror I passed.

I got the job at Bentall's, gave my name as Olivia G. Harris and wore my wig there every day.

At home, my parents soon got used to it. Dad thought I looked fantastic. Mum was more reserved. She said, "I just hope the wind doesn't blow too hard, that's all."

The new name was more difficult. I tried hard to wean my family away from Gladys, but it didn't really work. As Dad explained, "We've been calling you Gladys for twenty years now, Glad. We can't start calling you Olivia, just like that."

In the circumstances, I didn't dare invite anyone home. This was a pity, because, in a couple of months, I met the man of my dreams, James, and was dying to show him off. It wasn't that he was madly handsome, but he had these sexy brown eyes that seemed to laugh and tease. And a mass of black hair with a wavy bit that kept falling over his forehead. Not least of his attractions was his aristocratic name – James Selby-Smith. Guess what he called me? Goldilocks!

After only four weeks of meeting James, I knew I was in love with him. He must have felt the same about me for, soon afterwards, he proposed.

I was so over the moon, I couldn't bring myself to say, "I'd love to, James, darling, but my real name is Gladys, my hair is false and, without it, my face is the shape of the full moon." So I simply said, "I'd love to, James, darling," and left it at that.

I knew I'd have to come clean with him sooner or later, but I kept putting it off. I wondered if his love was strong enough to cope with a double-confession.

What made it especially hard was that James thought I was so honest. "I can't stand lies or sham," he said, as we drove home one evening after a film. "The character in that movie now, fibbing and pretending to be what she wasn't. That would put me right off a girl."

My heart pounded. I'd have to tread carefully.

"He's so straightforward, you see," I explained to Miranda, later that night. "That's what makes it difficult."

"Well, you can't leave it till the wedding-day," she said. "You won't get Aunt Lucy or Uncle Bill to call you Olivia. And think what a shock poor James will get when he finds that your hair comes off at night." She giggled.

I shuddered. James so admired what he believed was my hair. "It's gorgeous. Like spun gold," he'd say.

The weeks flew by. We planned to marry in six months time. James was anxious to have me meet his parents in Yorkshire. He also hinted it was time he met mine.

I would have been walking on air, were it not for the burden of my secret. I planned to let it out, bit by bit, to minimise the shock. In any event, something would have to happen soon, or I'd become a nervous wreck.

It did. But not in the way I intended. The following week, I invited James to dinner on the Wednesday to meet my parents. They were thrilled to bits and promised not to call me *Gladys*. By the end of that evening, I resolved to come out with it about my real name. If he took that well, I would progress later to the subject of wigs.

On the Tuesday, I sat waiting for James to phone, so we could fix up a time for the following evening. He didn't.

I was about to telephone him, when I found to my dismay that my mobile had stopped working. Damn! Before I had time to get to the landline phone, the doorbell rang.

"That'll be Paul," Miranda shouted from upstairs. "Open the door, will you, Glad?"

I went to the door. But it wasn't Paul standing outside. It was James.

"James!" I gasped. "What a surprise!"

He didn't rush forward to give me a hug, as I expected. Instead, he stood there staring at me and pushing back his hair. At last, he stammered, "I – I tried to phone but I think there's something wrong with your mobile ... and I don't have your landline number ..."

He was still staring. Then, it hit me. My wig! I didn't have my wig on. Clapping a hand over my head, I turned away, wanting to crawl into the large crack on our front-door step.

Soon, Miranda's voice torpedoed through my thoughts. "Gladys!" she yelled as she raced down the stairs. "Gladys!" she shouted again across the hall. By the time she had reached the front door, there could have been no doubt in James's mind that my name was Gladys.

"Oh – I thought you were Paul," Miranda said, giving him a dazzling smile. "Don't tell me. You're James."

James smiled back at her. I groaned inwardly. It was growing more like a nightmare every minute. Now Miranda was flirting with him. All ready to go out, she looked more than usually ravishing: sleek dark curls dancing on her shoulders, eyes teasing … And there was I beside her, oh, so mousy, so exposed without my wig. I wondered miserably if he would notice how flat the top of my head looked now that it had only my fine, wispy hair to cover it.

"Do come in, James, and have a drink with us," Miranda said.

"Sorry. I - I must get back."

He wasn't looking at me any more. His eyes were on Miranda.

"Pity. Still, we'll see you tomorrow night, won't we?"

"I'm afraid not." James flicked back his hair again and looked uncomfortable. "I've got to go to Manchester, you see. I'll probably be late getting back. I didn't know about it till today. Apologise to your parents for me, will you? Must go."

He hurried to his car.

I went in and slammed the door, feeling all finished up, like a cup of cold tea. He was going to dump me, I could tell.

The days dragged by with no word from James. I tried calling his flat on Miranda's mobile but there was no answer. On Saturday my mobile was okay again, thanks to Dad.

That's when I heard from him. He sounded tense.

"Thank heavens your phone's working now. I must speak to you, Olivia. I know it's short notice, but could we meet this afternoon and try to sort things out?"

Sort things out? I knew what that meant. I felt my world crumbling. He wanted to break off our engagement.

I tightened my lips. Well, let him. However hurt I felt, I wouldn't embarrass him by bursting into tears. I had my pride.

We met at our favourite cafe, the one with the red-checked cloths on the tables and strong aroma of coffee. James, who dressed casually as a rule, wore a grey suit which made him look older and more distinguished.

I felt a surge of longing and had to suppress an impulse to clasp his hand and beg him not to dump me.

He ordered coffee. Then he gazed across at me, brown eyes anxious. "I should have told you this before," he began. He paused and chewed his lip. He was afraid, I could tell, afraid to hurt my feelings.

Well, he needn't worry. "It's okay, I know already," I said. I tried to sound cool, but there was a lump in my throat, and my voice shook.

I fought to control myself. "You made it plain when you met me on Tuesday night that you wanted to break off our engagement."

I blew my nose and looked away, trying to compose myself.

The waitress came. When I turned to James again, he was pouring out the coffee. He said softly, "So it really *was* you I saw that night, was it, that divine little elf whose name turned out to be Gladys? I would have chatted with her longer, but she didn't seem that interested, so I thought I'd push off."

My mouth hung open. "You mean, you didn't think she was awful?"

He laughed. "Not at all. Different though, I must admit. I was dumbstruck."

His expression grew anxious again. "I meant to ask her how she'd like living in Manchester."

My heart leapt. He wasn't going to dump me then.

"You see, I've been chosen to manage our new branch there. That's what I wanted to talk to you about."

He looked up, his eyes gleaming. "It would give our marriage such a good start, Olivia. My income would be double what it is now – we could get a house straight away."

I couldn't speak for the wave of relief that flooded over me. We were still engaged. He didn't mind Gladys or her wispy hair.

"Of course, I know you love London. And Manchester is a long way away. But you will think about it, won't you?"

I laughed with joy. "I've already thought. And I will come."

His face lit up.

On the way home, I murmured, "Sorry I deceived you – about my hair, and everything."

James chuckled. "Don't worry, Goldilocks. You didn't quite fool me. I couldn't get that close to you without guessing you wore a wig. What took me by surprise was how different you look without it. It's as if I'm marrying two girls, not one." His voice softened. "Did you think I'd dropped you, just because

I saw you with your own hair? I'm not that shallow, I hope."

I bit my lip. "I wasn't sure. I'm hardly the beauty of the family. And there's my name …" I snuggled up to him. "You will go on calling me Olivia?"

"If you want. You should keep Gladys too, though, to save complications. It's a perfectly respectable name. I've an aunt called Gladys."

I grinned. "I bet you have."

"She's a hairdresser," he added. "An excellent one. She'd work wonders with your hair – even though her name's Gladys."

He went on, "If you'd been born with a name like mine, you'd have had something to moan about."

I frowned. "Why? What's wrong with James Selby-Smith?"

"Nothing. Except it wasn't the name I was born with. Selby-Smith was my mother's maiden-name. I was born – wait for it – James Albert Scrubber." He sighed. "Terrible, isn't it?"

I gasped. There I'd been, worrying myself silly because I'd deceived him about my name, while all the time … I'd have been angry, if it hadn't struck me as funny too. So I was going to be Mrs Scrubber!

James drew up outside my front door, pulled me to him and said with a twinkle. "Don't worry. I changed it by deed poll. I wouldn't inflict my wife with a name like that."

I kissed him. "I'd have put up with it anyway," I said. "After all, what's in a name?"

PLUM PUDDING

(An Old-fashioned Fairy Story with a Modern Theme)

Long ago, in the kingdom of Barania, there lived three princesses. The two older ones were slinky-slim like models. The youngest, however, was so plump and round *she* looked more like a large tea-cosy. This was a pity, for in Barania in those days fashion ruled that thin was `in' and stout was `out'.

"What are we to do about poor Belinda?" sighed the Queen one day as she watched the fat little princess charge like a young elephant through the royal sitting-room. "Soon, she'll be seventeen, old enough to sit in the royal processions. And then what will we do?"

"Do, my dear? What do you mean, do?" asked the King, mildly, over the top of his newspaper.

"Oh, use your head!" snapped the Queen. "Think what a ridiculous figure she'll cut next to Esmiralda and Isabel in the Royal Carriage. She'll look like the pastry-cook got in by mistake."

The King tut-tutted into his beard. "You fuss too much, my dear," he said. "Belinda's fine. A bit on the stout side perhaps. But what of it? In my young days, stoutness was very well thought of."

"In your young days," returned the Queen, "most of the rest of us weren't even born, so it hardly counts."

Her manner grew more and more cross. "Do you know what they are calling her down in the kitchen?"

She glanced furtively round the room, then whispered, "Plum Pudding, that's what."

The King turned pale. This was serious. Nicknaming a royal princess suggested contempt for the Crown. And contempt could lead to revolution. It must be stopped.

At first he thought of stopping it by Act of Parliament, but after more thought, decided to send for the Royal Physician, Dr Coff. "Have you a special medicine for curing fatness?" he asked.

"Diet and exercise, your Majesty, are the only cures," Dr Coff replied with a bow. "I can guarantee a distinct improvement within six weeks, if you will allow me to prescribe …"

Belinda soon found her routine greatly upset. There were no more nice, cosy lessons in Embroidery or Painting with her favourite governess, Miss Chat. Instead, she was taught the three Js: Jerking, Jogging and Jumping. Each morning a muscly lady with large teeth and well-scrubbed face came striding into the classroom saying breezily, "Come along, come along! Time for our exercises! Feet astride, head up, tummy in." There followed hours of bending, stretching and jumping, till Belinda felt as worn-out as a galley-slave.

Less arduous but more embarrassing to the princess was her afternoon jog in her blue shorts. She knew the shorts caused no end of amusement among palace officials who often strolled by as she puffed her way round the palace.

After all this tiresome running about there was nothing Belinda longed for more than a good roast lunch. But she soon found that Dr Coff's special diet was even more disagreeable than his exercises.

"For effective and speedy weight reduction," he told the Queen, "give her Royal Highness grapefruit for breakfast, raw carrot and tomato for lunch, and nothing for supper. Also, no buttered toast, no bacon and egg and definitely no chocolate cake."

And so, each day, tired and hungry, Belinda sat at the luncheon-table, nibbling raw carrot while her sisters munched away at their roast beef and potatoes. How she hated Dr Coff and his treatment!

The worse of it was, she seemed to grow no thinner. At the end of six weeks she was still plump and round like a tea-cosy. The Queen was furious and screamed, "Send for the physician!"

Dr Coff arrived, trembling in his shoes. "It m-must be her g-glands," he stammered.

In fact, as Belinda well knew, the problem was a steady stream of mince pies which, out of her own pocket money, she had bribed the royal kitchen to supply. The King, of course, was unaware of this and gave the unfortunate doctor a thorough dressing down. Afterwards, he confiscated his stethoscope, though he rejected the Queen's demands to confiscate his head as well.

With Dr Coff in disgrace, various magicians and mystics offered remedies but these were soon found to be hocus-pocus. "The only thing getting any slimmer," sighed the King, "is the Royal Purse." He failed to realise that the solution was to stop Belinda's pocket-money.

By this time, the whole family despaired of ever curing Belinda's fatness. They began to look upon her as a FAILURE and a LIABILITY.

Her sisters were particularly hurtful. Esmiralda made it plain that she was ashamed to be seen in Belinda's company, while Isabel mocked her with names like Jumbo and Humpty Dumpty.

Belinda gave as good as she got. "I'd sooner be an elephant than a scarecrow like you," she told her.

The only time she went out in a procession – and these were frequent in those days, with their majesties wearing crowns, and soldiers in full dress uniform – a rude boy shouted, "Hi there, Plum Pudding!" Roars of laughter followed, and even the troops found it hard to keep straight faces.

The King, now thoroughly alarmed, proceeded to what he called radical measures. He stopped Belinda's public appearances and banished her to a remote part of the palace with only her Pekinese for company. "You're a liability," her mother explained, while her father said, "Try to be philosophical about it."

Belinda made an effort to stay cheerful. "At least I have Ho-Ming and my painting to while away the time," she told herself. "And they're not starving me to death any more, thank goodness." Nevertheless, she felt lonely and a failure.

There were, however, Reasons of State for her banishment, over and above the Plum Pudding disaster. The King, visiting her, explained: "You've heard of Prince Oko of Okonga, my love? Well, we've invited him to the palace."

Belinda's face lit up. She'd seen pictures of Prince Oko. He was a dish.

"We hear he's looking for a wife," the King said, rubbing his hands, "somebody who'll bring him a decent dowry and an alliance with a powerful kingdom. Your mama thinks it would be a splendid opportunity for your sisters. As well as for the nut trade."

Belinda nodded. Okonga nuts, she knew, were important in the manufacture of plum-puddings for which Barania was, and still is, world famous.

"Prince Oko could hardly charge us such high prices if he became our son-in-law," her father went on. "But I'm forced to agree with the Queen that for our plans to succeed, we'll have to ... er ..." He paused and looked away. "...to *confine* you for a while. It might put him off, you see, my love, to find that Esmiralda and Isabel had an extra-plump sister. He'd assume that fatness ran in the family and could pass on to his own children."

Belinda felt tears sting her eyes. "Then I can't see him?"

The King gave her a hug. "Sorry, Sweetheart, but you'd best stay out of the whole thing."

Prince Oko's acceptance of their invitation was greeted with triumph and soon the whole palace was a hive of activity as preparations were made for balls, theatrical shows and garden-parties in honour of his visit.

The King paced up and down the palace, notebook in hand, giving instructions here, advice there. Meanwhile, the Queen fussed round her two elder daughters, like a hen with chicks. "Don't forget to wear your tightest girdles," she commanded. "And, whatever you do, don't frown and don't fidget."

Instructions like these, she decided, were most important, for Prince Oko was said to be discerning to a fault when it came to choosing a bride. He'd already met the Princess Ania and other celebrated beauties, but so exacting were his tastes that they failed to suit him. None of the family had ever visited Okonga, but they'd heard rumours that the ladies there were so beautiful that no one in the northern lands could compare with them.

This did nothing to weaken the Queen's confidence. "Just wait till he sees my daughters!" she told the King.

"Nuts," he said, "are an important factor in all this."

On the day of the prince's expected arrival, the two princesses were fitted out with new gowns full of frills and flounces. Their faces were painted, nails polished and hair curled, until, finally, the Queen said with a happy sigh, "You look like two flowers."

Belinda, of course, remained in her apartment and missed all the fun, though, to be fair, the King insisted she be allowed to watch the garden-party from an upper balcony of the palace.

"No way is that *all* I'll do," Belinda told herself, moving her chair to the window.

She kept her eyes skinned, and soon caught glimpses of Prince Oko. Her heart leapt. He was indeed handsome. Charming too, the way he listened politely to everyone, even to Isabel who, Belinda thought, was sure to be twittering on about clothes, or the latest ball.

As soon as she saw him walking alone, she cupped her hands over her mouth and called down "Cooee."

He stopped and looked around, but evidently couldn't see her. So she threw down a hankie with *Belinda* embroidered in the corner.

Seeing it fluttering down, he leapt forward, grabbed it, and gazed upwards. At the same moment, a group of palace officials appeared behind him.

"Dash it!" Belinda muttered, and quickly shut her window.

The Queen, meanwhile, was confident a proposal was on the way, but the King was more doubtful. He noticed that whenever he brought up the subject of his daughters and their many qualities, the Prince would promptly start talking about nut-farms.

Princess Belinda went on watching from her window. The next time she caught sight of Prince Oko walking below, she opened it, gave a loud whistle and this time threw down a note. It landed on the prince's shoulder. He plucked it off and read it. It said: *Save me, dear prince – Belinda.*

He was about to investigate when he heard the King calling. "Oko, wait!"

The King took his arm. He had decided that the best way to secure an alliance was to impress the young man with a grand tour of the palace.

With this in mind, he led him inside. He began with the ground floor, mentioning casually the value of the furniture as they passed through Rooms of State and pointing to the wall-safe where the crown jewels were kept with the remark, "It's really too small. Unless my daughters get married and take their share of the diamonds, I shall have to get a bigger one."

The Prince nodded and walked on and up, admiring the famous frescoes, the ballroom, the chandeliers above the Grand Staircase.

But his mind was on other matters. He couldn't wait to get to the top floor.

When they reached the last flight of stairs, however, the king laid a restraining hand on his arm. "There's nothing more to see, sweet prince."

Oko frowned. That handkerchief, plus the note, had come floating down from a top-floor window. He was sure that was where the unfortunate Belinda was imprisoned. "Please let me visit the upper rooms, Sire," he pleaded, beginning to climb.

The King stroked his beard, nervously. "Very well, but they're mostly empty." He hurried the young man along the top corridor, wincing at the way he threw open each door and peered inside. As they approached room number 1006, the King tightened his grip on the prince's arm and tried to pull him away. "Right. That's the lot."

The prince shook himself free and rattled at the door. It was locked but there came a faint cry from within. He stared accusingly at the King. "Surely, that's a maiden weeping?"

"Only a relative, er very distant," the King murmured, turning away, hastily. "She has an unfortunate disorder – extremely catching," he added.

Prince Oko narrowed his eyes. There was an unmistakeable look of guilt on the King's face. He remembered the old story of Bluebeard and resolved that before agreeing to any alliance, he would find out who was behind that door.

The King could see that his guest would not take even the politest no for an answer so, with a shrug of resignation, he opened the door. The Prince followed him inside, noting with relief that, at least, the room was comfortably furnished.

Then he saw Belinda. She was sitting in an armchair by the window, weeping all over her sketches of Pekinese dogs. Seeing her father, she wiped her eyes, hastily, curtsied and rushed into his arms. "Oh, Papa, you've come at last."

The King was much embarrassed at being caught out so completely in a fib. He searched his mind for an excuse, but was much affected by the thought that, fat or not, his youngest daughter was a pretty girl. Finally, he said, "Belinda, this is Prince Oko of Okonga, our state guest."

Belinda curtsied very low and once again saw under her long eyelashes, what a handsome young man he was.

And Prince Oko, bowing in a courtly manner, was quick to notice how extremely blue Belinda's eyes were and how delightfully her lips curved upwards as she smiled. But what finally captured his heart was her plump expanse of shoulder. As the princess blushed at his frankly admiring gaze, he said to the King, "Sire, your third daughter overwhelms me."

"I suppose she is rather overwhelming," the King agreed, sadly, "but she's a sweet girl underneath."

"Sweet and adorable," the prince said, softly, his eyes dreamy with love. "So modest and comely and so nicely rounded, she might be one of our Okonganese ladies.

Quite different from your other daughters who, if I may say so, look as if they haven't seen a good dinner in weeks."

The King couldn't believe his ears. "You mean – you don't find her too fat?" he faltered.

"I find her just right," Prince Oko replied. "Your ladies here are so scrawny, if you'll forgive my saying so. They'd be taken for beggar-women in my land. Belinda is a jewel and I want her for my wife." He held out his hand to Belinda who with, tears of joy on her cheeks, clasped it.

The King, pinching himself to make sure it wasn't a dream, embraced his future son-in-law and decided there and then to pass a new Act of Parliament for bringing plumpness back into fashion, as in the old days.

On the following Tuesday, Prince Oko, who would one day be King Oko, and Princess Belinda who would, one day, be Queen Belinda, were married amidst great festivity and rejoicing. And in the grand procession from the church the crowds cheered and threw flowers at the royal couple and no one spoilt it by yelling out, "Hi there, Plum Pudding!"

THE BLACK PORCELAIN HORSE

I should never have come. Attending Amy's funeral is one thing. Accepting Angela's request to join the others back at the house afterwards is quite another.

There's no sign of Angela now. She's probably behind in the kitchen making sandwiches with her daughter, Jess. I don't know anyone here and I'm feeling awkward, trying to balance a cup of tea on my lap while eating a sandwich.

I'd like to bolt, but opposite me, barring my way of escape sits a woman of about eighty or ninety, wearing a black hat with a silver ornament attached, shaped like a pony. It wobbles each time she moves her head. She has a small, scrunched-up face and petulant mouth. For half an hour she's cornered me here, twittering on and on about that black porcelain horse.

It appears she's Amy's cousin. She doesn't ask who *I* am. She's too absorbed in the horse question to wonder about me.

"I don't understand it," she whinges for about the fourth time. "I know it's not a thing one should talk about at a funeral, but Amy promised it to *me*, not to some young miss who isn't even related." She shakes her head and the decoration on her hat bobs about ominously. "Amy and I were so close, more like sisters than cousins, especially when we were children…"

I try to sooth her. "Perhaps she's left you something more valuable."

She dismisses my words with a flap of her hand. "I don't *want* anything more valuable. All I wanted was the horse." Her tone softens and her eyes take on a faraway look. "It's the memories, you see, the associations." She heaves a sigh and takes a sip of tea. "Angela told me I could take any ornament I fancied as a memento. Naturally, I asked for the horse. `Oh, you're too late for that, I'm afraid, Auntie Dor,' she said. `My mother gave it to Maggie, her care worker'."

Her hand trembles, and she spills some of her tea into her saucer. "I didn't say anything but … well … giving it away to a slip of a girl like that. To her it would just a piece of china to stick on a shelf and forget about."

She takes a handkerchief from the pocket of her black jacket and blows her nose. "It was more than a piece of china to me. It was our *past*, our memories."

She turns away. Her thin shoulders quiver and her mouth puckers up.

I feel a twinge of pity, a pang of unease. She looks so crushed, so pushed-aside somehow. I try to comfort her. "I'm sure your cousin meant to keep her promise," I say, "but being so confused those last few months, she forgot. I dare say she gave it to the care worker on impulse, maybe as a thank-you for some extra work she'd done."

She glares at me. "A thank-you indeed! The care worker was just doing her job. What *I* did for Amy, I did out of love."

Her voice breaks. Oh dear, I seem to have made things worse. Her eyes are beginning to glisten and I notice a tear fall into her cup.

"But it isn't that so much," she goes on, her voice steadying. "It's the bond we had as children, through our love of horses." The far-away look returns, giving her features an altogether softer cast. "We used to ride together for miles. In all weathers. We rode in competitions, you know." A look of pride floods her face. "My father was so impressed with us once, he presented us each with a black porcelain horse. It was a replica of our favourite stallion, Bold."

I frown. "But if you already have a statue of the horse?"

She shakes her head sadly, and the silver pony in her hat gets another fit of trembling. "It broke," she says. "Eight years ago. Matthew, my grandson..."

She goes into a long explanation.

I feel my eyes glaze over. I'm sorry for her but I'm growing tired of this one-sided conversation. I prepare to rise, but that pang of unease starts gnawing at me again. I listen to the rest of her lament.

"… And what do you think Angela said when I told her about Amy's promise?" She clutches at her throat, her lips pressed together so tightly they almost disappear.

I wait.

"She said, `Surely, Dor, you're not fussing about that old horse of Mum's. It's not *worth* anything'. I felt choked. `It's worth a lot to me,' I told her. `It's a symbol of our riding days'."

She swallows and looks down at her feet. "Angela only laughed. `God, Auntie, I believe you're still hankering after riding again. You're well past that, I'm afraid'."

She sniffs into her handkerchief. "I know I'm past it. But she needn't have rubbed it in." She turns her face to the window and gazes out into the distance. "You never forget it, you know, galloping through those fields, with the wind in your hair, jumping fences, rubbing the horses down afterwards, smelling the stables… So much freedom …" Her voice begins to tremble. "You still miss it, however old you are."

I feel a lump rise to my throat. "*I* don't think you're past it."

Her eyes are still watery but she manages a smile. "Thank you, my dear."

She's not a bad sort, I think. She's just desperate to hold on to a memory, a memory that was precious to her.

A plan starts to form in my mind. It's a bit naughty, but I'm determined to see more of that smile.

I clap a hand to my forehead, putting on a show of sudden recollection.

"I've just remembered… something I heard from Maggie, Amy's care worker."

She looks across at me, eyebrows raised.

"You did say your name was Doris?"

She nods.

I take a deep breath. "Well, Maggie said that your cousin gave the horse to her, not for her to *keep*, but to look after for Doris, because Doris would cherish it."

"You're serious?" Her eyes widen.

"Of course. The penny's only just dropped, that's all. Amy gave it to her, to keep safe for *you*, so that when she died, no one else would get her hands on it."

Her expression is a curious mixture of joy and doubt.

"So you know this girl, Maggie?"

"Quite well. In fact, I'm seeing her later today. She'll be only too pleased to hand over the horse, so I can pass it on to you later today. It will save her delivering it herself."

"Really? That's wonderful."

I've convinced her. She breaks into a smile which lights up her whole face. "I knew my dear Amy wouldn't forget me."

I take her wrinkled hand and give it a squeeze. "You'll miss your cousin, I'm sure, but the horse will remind you of the good times you had together."

"Oh, they will indeed. It was the image of Bold you know." Still smiling, she leans forward and pats my arm. "You're a nice, sensible girl. And so kind." She rises to her feet. "I must just visit the bathroom. After that, I shall see Angela and David and apologise for being such a silly old woman." She puts her cup and saucer on the coffee-table and reaches for her handbag. "Sorry to desert you, dear, but we'll be meeting later, won't we?"

With that she's off, looking as happy as if she'd just won the lottery. I watch her with satisfaction. I'm glad I told her that fib. At least it was in a good cause. I think back to my last meeting with Amy Boyd. "You've been so good to me, Maggie, dear, doing my shopping and everything," she'd said. "I'd like you to take one of these porcelain pieces to show my appreciation."

I chose the horse.

She hadn't meant to snub her cousin, I'm sure. But she had memory lapses. For a moment, she'd forgotten her promise. That was all.

I shall have a quick word with Angela. She mustn't spill the beans to Doris about who I am. It would spoil everything for her to find out that *I'm* that slip of a girl, Maggie, and that the horse was meant for me to keep. She has her pride.

I'm feeling easier now. And though I'll be sad to give up the little horse, the look on Doris's face when she finally holds it in her hands will more than make up for the loss.

DEJEUNER SUR L'HERBE

The setting for this story is Paris in the 1860s.
The characters are fictionalised but the background,
including Manet's rejected painting are based on fact

The drawing-room clock struck seven and, to Louise, seated at her embroidery-frame, the sound was ominous. Papa was late. Not that she looked forward with eagerness to his arrival – far from it. But at least she and her sister would know the worst, and anything, she decided, was better than this interminable waiting.

She threw her younger sister a reproachful glance. Lysette, angelic in white muslin, was draped over the chaise-longue, her head resting on the brocaded cushion, her hair like a golden cloud billowing round her. She lay pale and solemn-faced, eyes gazing upwards, seemingly engrossed in the chandelier above her head. If ever looks were deceptive, Louise thought, then Lysette's certainly were. For Lysette was no angel.

The younger woman stirred at last and sat up, a frown lining her forehead. "Why is Papa so late?

"Oh, I dare say he's at Le Coque D'Or drinking with Monsieur Meslier and Pierre," Louise replied, as casually as she could. "They'll be busy discussing the Salon de Refuses, I've no doubt, and arguing about the rejected pictures."

"Including Eduard Manet's, I suppose." With a sigh, Lysette rose to her feet. "Oh, Louise, what *am* I to do?" She drifted to the window and peered out.

"Perhaps there's no harm done. From what you've told me of the *Dejeuner sur L'Herbe*, it will be hung in some obscure corner of the salon where no one will notice it. Any sign of Papa?"

Her sister shook her head and began to pace the room, all the while fanning herself with an elegant lace fan. "If that old gossip, Meslier, has seen it, heaven knows what stories he'll spread all over Paris. As for Pierre ..." She broke off and, with a tragic gesture, flung down the fan and covered her face with her hands. "Oh, Louise, I'm a ruined woman. I shall kill myself."

"Don't be absurd. And keep your voice down. You'll disturb Mama." A twinge of irritation lent a sharp edge to Louise's voice. Was it merely her fancy, or was Lysette, beneath the anxious eyes and wringing hands, secretly revelling in her role of the fallen woman?

She stifled the ungenerous thought and said, comfortingly, "It's probable that no one will recognise you. After all, Monsieur Manet is a most incompetent painter, by all accounts. According to Papa, if he were a *poor* man, dependent on his pictures for a living, he'd die of starvation. He's done nothing of consequence for an age, not since *The Spanish Guitarist*."

"But if I *am* recognised?" Lysette sank into a nearby chair. "There'll be such a scandal."

"You should have thought of that before." Louise dug the needle hard into her embroidery-cloth. "You've shamed us over and over again with your thoughtless escapades," she scolded. "And now this:

posing in that lewd way, like a common street woman ... I – I blush for you."

Lysette sprang to her feet, pink with indignation. "But it wasn't my fault. You must believe me."

"I'm trying to, but the whole story sounds so improbable, I doubt if anyone will believe you. In any case, you were hardly blameless. What were you thinking of, wandering alone in a strange wood, and then, if you please, stripping off your clothes and bathing in a stream?"

Lysette gave an exasperated sigh. "I've already told you. It was stiflingly hot. The place seemed deserted. How was I to know that Monsieur Manet - who's excessively handsome, by the way - would appear out of nowhere, steal my clothes and refuse to return them, unless I promised to pose for him?"

Louise snorted. "Oh, come, Lysette. There are plenty of women of a certain class only too eager to pose for painters like Eduard Manet. Why should he go to such lengths and use such devious means to procure *you* as his model?"

"He told me I looked like Aphrodite. Perhaps that's why."

Louise rolled her eyes. "Some men will say anything to get what they want. Had you gone straight to Papa and told him, he would have put a stop to the whole monstrous business."

"How could I, without my clothes? Besides, you know Papa's temper ..."

Lysette broke off and stood still, listening. A rumble of carriage wheels could be heard drawing up outside the house. "It's Papa," she gasped and ran to her sister who, forgetting her anger, jumped up from her seat and placed a comforting arm around her waist.

Together they moved to the window and looked out. Below, a tall, middle aged man in a top hat was climbing out of an elegant Victoria. As he did so, he glanced briefly up at the drawing-room window where the two sisters hovered. Louise's heart sank as she observed her father's stern gaze. "Oh dear, he's frowning, and tugging at his beard," she murmured.

"Not good signs."

Soon, they heard the servant slamming the front door, the low boom of their father's voice in the hall, followed by the piping tones of their mother as, fresh from her nap, she hurried to greet him. Some moments later, they were in the drawing-room.

"Well, my dears, here's Papa at last, after an exhausting day at the salon. And my headache's quite gone now, thank goodness." Their mother smiled in a nervous, fluttery way, but her attempts at liveliness did not deceive Louise. No one could feel comfortable when Papa was out of temper.

He strode into the room, giving no more than a grunt by way of greeting. Then, he marched to the windows and flung them open. "This place is airless."

He turned and threw his daughters a withering look. "Are you so idle, you'd sooner bake than trouble yourselves with opening windows?"

"My fan kept me cool, Papa." Lysette opened it with a flourish.

He glowered at her, eyes glittering like ice-cubes. "I'd be happier, young lady, if you occupied yourself with something useful, like needlework, instead of lolling and posing, and waving that fan about."

Posing? Louise caught her breath. Did that mean …? She watched her father move, tight-lipped, towards his favourite armchair, snatch up the newspaper which lay awaiting him and begin to thumb his way through it.

Her mother, an anxious look on her face, hurried to the cocktail cabinet, and poured him a cognac. With scarcely a clink of the glass, she set it on the table beside him.

Louise coughed. It was unwise to interrupt her father in such a mood, but she *had* to find out what had happened. She took a deep breath and finally stammered, "And – er - how was the salon, Papa? Were there many people there?"

A growl emerged from behind her father's paper. "Far too many."

He said nothing more for a while, then went on, grudgingly, "All jostling and pushing to see the pictures. And the heat intolerable."

No one spoke for a few moments, as he scanned an article in *Le Matin,* and took a sip of cognac. Louise listened restlessly to the ticking of the clock, then probed again. "And was anyone important there, Papa?"

There followed an irritable rustling of newspaper as her father turned over the page. "Only the Emperor and Empress," he snapped, without looking up. "Otherwise, mostly riff-raff."

"Fancy! And how were the pictures, Papa?"

He gave her a sharp, narrow-eyed glance over his paper. "Since when, Louise, have you become so interested in art that you cannot allow your father to read in peace?"

She fell silent.

His lips stretched into a grim smile. "If you must know, they were, in the main, lamentable, a blot on the art world." He flapped his paper, noisily. "One, indeed, was in such bad taste, Napoleon was moved to strike it with his cane."

"Really? And what did the Empress do?" Mama gasped, curiosity overcoming timidity.

"Damn me, woman, what did you expect her to do?" With a gesture of impatience, her husband tossed aside his paper and glared at her. "She turned away, of course, and pretended not to see it."

"But what picture could have caused such a stir, Papa?" Louise faltered.

Her father's jaw tightened. "If you must know, a revolting piece of nonsense called the *Dejeuner sur L'Herbe*, or some such thing. By that degenerate painter, Manet. You should have heard the jeers." He twisted his lips into tight lines of disapproval. "Of course, there were those such as Baudelaire only too ready to jump to its defence. `Progressive Art', they called it." He leaned back in his chair and snorted. "Progressive Art! `Tasteless' would have been nearer the mark."

His voice hardened as he turned his gaze to Lysette. "As for the model … when, to all appearances, she is a commonplace woman of dubious morals, as one critic put it, the result is bound to be squalid."

Lysette averted her eyes, while her sister visibly quaked. He could surely not say such dreadful things about his own daughter?

"Of course, it was easy to see who she was." Papa gave one of his dramatic pauses as he folded his paper and slapped it down on the coffee-table.

The two sisters waited, Louise hardly daring to breathe.

He gave a thin smile and rose to his feet. "Ah, yes. That vile woman, Victorine Meurent."

Louise dropped her scissors with a clatter. There was surely some mistake. If Lysette had posed for the *Dejeuner sur L'Herbe*, then why ...

A sudden gleam of suspicion crossed her mind as, glancing at her sister, she noticed how totally unruffled she appeared to be. Her face darkened. Had Lysette made the whole thing up simply to amuse herself and vex her sister? Was she secretly thrilled at the idea of being the talk of Paris? Ah, well, she would soon find out. She would confront that minx of a sister and demand an explanation.

This turned out to be no easy task.

Time after time, when alone with Lysette, Louise strived to question or coax out the truth, but Lysette showed a strange reluctance to discuss the matter. A secret smile or a swift change of subject was all she would offer by way of response.

With a sigh, Louise gave up, certain at last that her sister's story was indeed utterly false, and her behaviour mere play-acting.

Some years later, this certainty began to waver.

She chanced one day to see at an art exhibition a study by Manet for the *Dejeuner sur L'Herbe*. This small picture contained only the nude, and Louise was curious to note that the model had fair hair, not dark, and that her features, unlike Victorine Meurent's, were soft and demure.

She drew in a sharp breath and studied the picture more closely. The body was a shade too rounded perhaps. But the braided hair ... and that reflective look in the eyes ... It was unmistakable.

Her heart began to race.

"No one knows the identity of the model," they informed her at the gallery. "She's a mystery."

"Not to me," Louise murmured softly, gazing once more at the girl in the picture. "Not to me."

THE PIANO TEACHER

When Amy Rawson came to live in Oak Lane, I guessed there'd be trouble. Though well into her forties, she looked a real man-eater: glossy black hair, eye-lashes to die for, and curves in all the right places. On top of that, she was unattached, and drove a Porsche.

"She's not short of a bob or two," Brenda next door told me with a confidential wink. "No wonder. She's a funeral director. You can't lose with a job like that."

I didn't see much of her for the first couple of weeks. Then one day, without warning, she appeared on our doorstep.

"Hullo, I'm Amy, just moved into the corner house." She spoke in a breathy voice and flashed me a smile, revealing a set of dazzling-white teeth.

I thought she'd come merely to introduce herself or ask about the village.

"We've not lived in Bucksfield long ourselves," I said. "And we don't know many people yet, apart from Brenda and Cliff next door and the Bryants across the road, who keep all those chickens…"

She gave a polite cough. "Actually, I'm looking for someone called Patrick."

I grew wary. "That's my husband."

"Ah, I've come to the right house then. Your next-door neighbour tells me he gives piano-lessons."

"News to me," I said.

Strains of the Appassionata came pounding out from the sitting-room. Pat, at the piano again, murdering Beethoven.

"You'd better come in and see him," I sighed.

Pat, full of smiles, rose from the piano-stool to greet her. "I'll be delighted to teach you," he said.

I tightened my lips. Talk about eager!

Warning bells rang in my brain. It's not that I don't trust my husband. But the thought of this woman, with her plunging neckline and sexy chain-belt, cosily installed in our sitting-room with him, for an hour-long lesson …. Anyway, what did *he* know about teaching music?

She turned up the following evening for her first lesson. I stayed in the kitchen, washing dishes. From what I could make out, they spent more time nattering than working on chords or scales. Pat *did* play a couple of piano pieces to show off his skill. But, apart from that, all I could hear was the odd rumble of conversation mixed with shrieks of laughter from Amy.

I've never known anyone laugh so much. Perhaps, I thought, I'd better enter the funeral business myself. It might lighten me up a bit. Just now, I felt in need of some lightening up. I'm not normally a jealous person but it made me seethe to find myself stuck with the dishes in the kitchen, while those two had a great time, laughing and joking. I couldn't hear any piano practising. What the hell were they up to?

"Nice girl," Pat commented, after seeing her out. "Good sense of humour. And she likes my playing." He smiled in a self-satisfied sort of way.

She came for another lesson later in the week, and again, on Wednesday of the week following. This time, after the lesson had ended, Pat invited me into the sitting-room for a drink with them. Big deal, I thought. I did my best to be polite and chatty but found it hard to disguise the chill in my mood. I could tell she didn't feel at ease with me. I wasn't too comfortable with her either. What do you talk about to a funeral director?

"I'm taking Amy into Chesham on Saturday to find her a piano," Pat told me later. "Want to come?"

"Are you sure I won't be in the way?" I asked, my voice heavy with sarcasm.

"Don't be silly. I *want* you to come." He put an arm round me. "Let me play my new Chopin piece to you. It's one of your favourites."

"No thanks. I've heard enough thumping on the piano for one evening."

He dropped his arm and turned away.

I shouldn't have said that. He didn't always thump. There were times when I loved his playing. But I wasn't in the mood for dishing out compliments.

I decided I *would* go piano-hunting with them, if only to keep an eye on things. I didn't trust that woman.

I'd heard from Brenda lurid details about her sexual proclivities. Brenda had heard about them from George, the postman, who never missed the chance of a gossip. Amy had apparently opened the door to him one morning, clad only in a transparent nightie. "You could see *everything*," he told Brenda, drooling.

Brenda told me that she and Cliff had once spotted her, dressed in nothing but a pair of shorts, mowing her back lawn. "Good thing my Cliff's so unobservant," she giggled. "All he said was, `She shouldn't be gardening in bare feet like that. She might step on a thorn'."

You can see what I was up against. A real siren. And fancy starting piano lessons without even having a piano!

The following Saturday, Amy went with Pat to buy one. And, of course, I tagged along too, feeling more like a gooseberry in this threesome than anything else. I yawned and sighed, like a sulky ten-year-old, as we searched for the music-shop.

They didn't seem to notice. Too busy jawing. Pat was airing his views on modern composers such as Michael Tippet, and rattling on about the merits of a Bluthner Grand as opposed to a Steinway. Amy listened attentively, responding now and then with cries of "Really?" and, "How marvellous!" Each utterance followed, of course, by her usual trills of laughter.

At the music-shop, Amy flitted from piano to piano, admiring this one, then that one, Pat, close at her side, acting the connoisseur. I heard him run his hands along the keys of each one, to make sure it was properly tuned. I watched, eyes glazing over, as he peered at the woodwork and questioned the salesman about its condition. After more than an hour, he gave Amy his advice on the best choice. She took it.

I breathed a sigh of relief. At last!

"I hope you're charging for her piano lessons," I said, after we arrived home.

"Oh no. I couldn't possibly."

"Why not? You've spent enough time on her. And you're always complaining about what little time you've got. Anyway, she's not exactly hard-up."

"Don't be so mercenary. I do it because I enjoy it. Besides, I could hardly *charge*. I'm not qualified."

I wondered about that. What the hell had made Brenda recommend Pat in the first place? I'd have to have it out with her.

It was what happened the following day that finally decided me. Pat had gone to the Garden Centre and spent ages there. When he got back, he announced, "I've just been having a chat with Amy in her garden."

"I hope she had something more than shorts on," I snapped.

He ignored my sarcasm. "I thought it would be nice to take her to that Mahler concert with us on Thursday evening. I could easily get an extra ticket."

I almost burst a blood-vessel.

"You don't mind, do you? She's all on her own. She needs a few friends."

"I'll *bet*." I shot him a filthy look, banged the sitting-room door, and stalked out into the kitchen. There, I started crashing saucepans about.

He followed me in. "What's the matter with you? Amy's new to the area and so are we. I thought you and she might become friends. Don't you like her?"

"No, I don't. And she doesn't like me." I plonked myself down on a kitchen chair, arms folded, lips pursed. "And if *she's* going to the concert on Thursday, you can count me out."

Patrick lifted his eyes to heaven. "You're acting like a spoilt child. And it's ridiculous to say Amy doesn't like you. She *does*. She thinks you're – sweet."

I winced. *Sweet*!

"Anyway, I've already invited her now."

"Then uninvite her."

"I can't do that." It was his turn to bang the door and stalk out.

I gritted my teeth. I'd put a stop to this liaison somehow. I was sick of Amy with her glamorous looks, her Porsche, and her trills of laughter. And how dare she call me `sweet'?

Later that day, I popped next door to see Brenda.

She was pottering in the kitchen, making lemon-tarts. "For my grandchildren," she explained. "Have one. Can't touch them myself, not with my figure." She spread out her arms. "Look at me. Size of a house. And I eat like a bird."

I came quickly to the point. "It's about Amy. I wondered why you recommended *Patrick* to give her piano lessons."

She frowned. "Why not? He's a professional piano-teacher."

"You've got it wrong, Brenda," I said. "He plays the piano, yes, but he'd never given a lesson in his *life*, before Amy came …"

I stopped. Brenda, who'd been frowning and gaping at me in turn, broke out into a gale of laughter.

"I don't believe it!" she finally gasped. "Do you mean to say, Amy's coming to *your* Patrick for her piano lessons?"

I nodded.

"The daft ha'porth. I suggested Patrick Bryant across the road. I even pointed out the house.

"Oh, I didn't realise … I thought the Bryants just kept chickens." My heart lifted. "I'd better explain to

Amy. I'm sure Patrick – *my* Patrick, I mean - wouldn't want to give her lessons under false pretences."

I stepped into my own house, creased up with laughter. I couldn't wait to phone Amy.

Before I could do so, *she* phoned us.

"I'll have to abandon my lessons for the time being," she said. "There's a lot of work coming in. I'm going to be terribly busy. And I can't make Thursday, after all, I'm afraid. Sorry to mess you about."

Perhaps she'd heard from Brenda about her blunder, I thought, and was too embarrassed to face us again. Or perhaps she really *was* busy. Maybe the current heat wave had caused an increase in fatalities.

Pat took the news stoically, but I could tell he was disappointed.

We saw little of Amy after that, other than to catch a glimpse of her red Porsche disappearing up Oak Lane.

A few months later, she disappeared from the village altogether. Brenda told me she'd left for Switzerland, at midnight, in a van. Nobody knew why, or what she was doing about her funeral business.

"A bit fishy, isn't it?" I said, "leaving like that in the middle of the night?" I had a gratifying vision of the police on her trail for some hideous crime such as nicking gold rings from her dead clients and melting them down for profit. "D'you think the police were after her?"

"Of course not," Brenda answered in shocked tones.

She lowered her voice. "More like she's fleeing from her ex. He's been pestering her again, and there's an injunction against him." She shook her head, gravely. "He treated her very badly, you know. Gave her hell, for years."

I shooed away my unkind fantasy and murmured, "Poor Amy!"

More subdued I made my way back to the house to tell Patrick the news.

He said, "I guessed she was hiding a problem or two, behind all that laughter."

"She was very attractive," I ventured.

He shrugged. "I didn't really notice. She was nice, though. And she liked my playing."

So that's what it was all about, I thought. She'd shown an interest in his piano-playing. Something I'd seldom done. And we all like a bit of appreciation now and again.

"She had good taste," I said. I clasped his hand, a feeling of tenderness welling up inside me. "Play some Schubert. I loved that piece you played this morning."

His eyes began to glisten. "Did you? Honestly?" He squeezed my hand, and something like joy crossed his face as he sat on the piano-stool and began to play.

DROPPING OUT

When I told Mac, our glider-pilot friend, that we'd signed up for a parachuting course, his eyes nearly popped out. "Parachuting course? At your age? Planning to kill yourselves, are you?" A grin started at the corners of his mouth. "Anyway, how will you cope with jumping from a plane? I'm told you freak out even at the thought of driving a car."

I gave him a dirty look. "You can get killed driving a car." I said. With a shudder, I remembered my last driving-lesson. I'd almost knocked down a cyclist, and very nearly killed myself and my driving instructor at the same time. Confidence shattered, I'd cancelled my next lesson. At least, with parachuting, I thought, I was risking only my own life, not everyone else's as well.

Mac heaved a sigh. "You can get killed all sorts of ways," he agreed. "But anyone jumping from a plane by choice wants his head read. It's a hell of a dangerous sport."

I rolled that over in my mind. If anyone knew about danger, Mac did. Time after time he'd taken risks with his glider and his powered aircraft. It seemed though he drew the line at parachuting.

His grin was gone now, his brow knotted with concern. "Don't do it. It's a mug's game."

I choked back the flutter of nervousness rising to my throat. Damn it! I wasn't going to back out now. Not when it was all arranged and paid for. Anyway, it was my birthday gift to Patrick, my husband. And Pat was crazy on the idea. I did have a more personal motive. I wanted to prove to myself that for once in my life, I'd do something that took guts. And who knows? If I dared to jump from an aircraft, I might eventually dare to drive a car again. I'd show that Mac I wasn't some ageing wimp.

When the time came, we stayed at the Shobdon Parachute Club overnight, so we could turn up on the dot for our one-day crash course the following morning. It was a beginners' course, starting at 8.30 in the morning and ending with the jump at 5.00 in the afternoon. Pat and I exchanged wry smiles as we scanned the rest of the group. We were the only senior citizens there. And I was the only woman. The others were all lads, sturdy, and ready for anything.

The morning's events started off with a lecture and discussion on the mechanics of parachuting. Not knowing the mechanics of anything, I surprised myself by asking a couple of intelligent questions. At least, that's what the instructor called them.

After this, things became more physical, with a long session of exercises such as press-ups, followed by intensive training in the techniques of parachute landing. One after another, we practised our falling, landing and rolling under the scrutiny of the coach.

"How much longer is this going on for?" Pat asked me with a sigh. "I'm puffed out. And I feel like a geriatric, trying to keep up with these youngsters."

"Look on the bright side," I said. "There's no time to get in a flap about the actual jump while we're so busy practising it."

But as the day wore on, I could feel myself getting more and more jittery. This feeling approached fever pitch when, in the middle of the afternoon, we had a lesson on emergency procedures – what to do, for example, if the parachute proved faulty.

"In this case, of course," the coach said, "you'll have to abandon it and pull the rip-cord to release your spare one."

"Suppose that's faulty too, or the rip-cord gets stuck and you can't pull it?" I whispered to Pat.

"Listen, and maybe you'll find out," he said.

The coach went on. "Again, there's the problem of an unexpected wind springing up and blowing you into a tree. The important thing here is to shield the face."

At this point I really began to lose nerve. The possibility of having a faulty parachute or of crashing into a tree set my whole body trembling. I began to pray that the drizzle that had started up would develop into a thunderstorm so that our jump would have to be postponed. I'd be spared then the shame of having to chicken out.

But the drizzle stopped. The sun came out, and at 5 o'clock Pat and I, rigged out in our parachute gear were standing with three of the others from our group, all ready to step into the small plane awaiting us.

My inside felt like jelly. So far, I had won the battle with my nerves. There was still time to disgrace myself, but I knew that, once on the plane, there was no backing out. If, at the last moment, I refused to jump, not only would I be letting myself and my sex down, I would also be letting down the group. Being the lightest, it was my job to jump first. If I didn't, then no one else could either for I'd be blocking their way to the exit-hatch. In my mind's eye I could see three disappointed young men fuming over their bad luck at being placed in a group with an elderly female who, predictably, copped out at the last moment.

"You feeling okay?" Pat asked, squeezing my hand as he helped me into the plane.

"Fine," I lied, making an effort to keep my voice steady. "Happy birthday."

There was very little room on the plane. We were huddled together like factory-farm chickens. I, being the first to make my exit, knelt near the doorway. At a signal from the coach I was to sit, facing it, my legs splayed out, a foot on each side of the opening, waiting for the order, "Jump!"

My teeth were chattering now as, through the exit-hatch, I could see the ground getting further and further away until soon only clouds were visible below me. I began to feel physically sick. "Give me a push when the time comes," I urged the pilot.

It's funny, but I can't seem to remember if I was pushed, or if I jumped. When I try to recall that crucial moment of dropping out, my mind remains a blank.

What is clear to me is the interval between that moment and the moment my parachute opened. It should have been the most nerve-shattering point in the course. But it wasn't. I was still nervous, of course, but now my anxiety was mingled with a kind of exhilaration and excitement. I felt not so much the sensation of hurtling down to earth, more the feeling of swimming through space.

At the same time, I had to follow instructions. First, I had to manoeuvre my body into the correct spread-eagle position. Not easy, with the wind buffeting me about. Also, I had to yell out the seconds: ten, nine, eight ….

On the seventh count, the parachute opened.

I breathed a sigh of relief. So far, so good. All I had to do now was grasp the wooden toggles and steer myself towards the landing place, marked with an orange cross.

It was at this point that I was faced with my first hitch. I couldn't *see* the landing place. A voice came over my radio: "Face the cross, number one!" I desperately scanned the panorama of fields and hills spread out below me but could see nothing I recognised, let alone the cross.

Over the radio, the voice came again, repeating the instruction. I began to sweat. Then, in dismay, I realised what was wrong. In my haste, I had put on my reading-glasses instead of my distance ones. No wonder everything below looked so hazy. The instructor tried a different tactic. "Pull your right toggle."

I did so but, although I was getting nearer and nearer the ground, I still couldn't make out in any detail what was below me. There was no sign of the orange cross and, whether it was a field of corn or a forest that was rushing up to meet me, I could not tell.

I got into the correct position for landing, closed my eyes and prepared for the crash which would surely knock me senseless, if it didn't kill me.

To my amazement, I met the ground with a gentle bump and sustained not even a graze. I had landed in a field of corn. I lay there a moment, elated. I'd done something dangerous, extravagant, rash. And I was still alive to tell the tale. After this, I thought, what are driving lessons? I would take them in my stride.

Admittedly, I had bungled the landing. Not that I was the only one. I later learned that one unlucky young man had dropped on the runway and broken his ankle. Another had fallen amongst a herd of cows who tried to eat his parachute! Pat, of course, landed bang in the middle of the cross. He would!

A few weeks after our return home we phoned Mac. I was eager to tell him that, having participated in `a hell of a dangerous sport' without mishap, I now felt quite relaxed about driving.

Sadly, we were never to chat or joke with Mac again. We later learned from the Gliding Club that he had been killed - in a car crash. His death, and the irony of it, stunned us. That Mac, who'd been so keen to point out the dangers of parachuting, should himself be killed – driving his *car*, seemed as unlikely an outcome as the contrived twist at the end of a tale.

We haven't repeated our parachuting adventure. For me, once is enough. Pat says he'd like another shot, but adds, "So long as I don't have to go through all those exercises again."

Yet, even if it turns out to be our last as well as our first experience, I'm glad I plucked up the courage to do it. It's done wonders for my ego.

I have to confess though that I still haven't learnt to drive. After hearing about Mac's accident, I cancelled my first lesson and I've yet to arrange another.

THE CHOCOHOLIC

It was two weeks before Christmas when I first discovered there were intruders in our loft.

I'd gone up to hunt for an old coat, one I'd worn in my mini-skirted days and had a sudden urge to wear again.

Not that it would do as a coat any more, I thought, as I clambered from the ladder onto the loft floor. Unless mutton-dressed-as-lamb was to be my new fashion statement. A white leather coat, trimmed with fur, and cut well above the knee, was hardly the in-thing for the mature woman. Still, worn as a jacket, over a sensible skirt or trousers, who knows?

I straightened. You can do this in our loft. It's huge, like a barn. The trouble is, it's *packed* with stuff. We're hoarders, Patrick, and I. Dismembered toys, torn bedding, scribbled-on books, up they come to wither and rot. There are lines of clothes on hangers, in boxes and sacks. "You never know," I tell myself." They might come back into fashion,"

It was going to take time and patience to find that coat.

I glanced to my left. As I did so, my mouth started watering. My Christmas chocolates were piled up there, together with early gifts from friends and relatives, probably chocolates too. A daft place to store them, I know, but kept downstairs, they'd never last till Christmas. Too easy for me to get at.

The trouble is, I'm a chocoholic. I'm making efforts to curb my addiction, especially as waistbands are getting hard to do up, and bulges developing in so many places. "Don't ask me if your bum looks big in those trousers," Patrick warns. "You might not like the answer."

Like it or not, I could *smell* those chocolates, and *taste* them. An imaginary piece filled with soft caramel toffee lay there on my tongue, waiting to be rolled around.

I felt my will power crumble and die. Perhaps, I thought, if I just check on the pile …

I stepped to my left, my salivary glands working overtime as I knelt down and peered into the shallow, open box displaying the chocolates.

That's when I let out a gasp. "Oh, *no!*" I felt a rush of blood to my head.

Every bar and box had been vandalised: wrappings torn off, boxes bitten into, half-eaten chocolate liqueurs, spilling their sticky contents over everything. A giant chocolate Santa had its silver tunic ripped to shreds, while its head was nowhere to be seen. Not a single item had remained untouched.

Forgetting the coat, I sprang to my feet and clumped down the loft-ladder, uttering threats of violence at every step.

My husband was working at his computer in the study.

"Who's been after my chocolates?" I demanded. "They're half-eaten."

"Don't look at me. I wouldn't dare." He got up. "Are you sure you haven't eaten them yourself?"

"Don't be stupid. I wouldn't eat my Christmas stuff."

"It must be mice then." He heaved a sigh. "That's *all* we need. Before Christmas too. We'll have to get the council in."

Mice. So *they* were the intruders. I should have guessed. I pulled a face. I was partial to most animals, but wasn't at all sure about mice. I didn't care for their pointy faces or long thin tails like worms.

"How will they get rid of them?" I asked.

Pat shrugged. "Put down poison, I expect."

"That's horrible," I said. "They might be little thieves but I don't want them suffering."

Pat put on his thinking look. "There are humane traps," he said at last. "You stick in something tasty. Mouse makes a dive for it, and, wham, door shuts, and you've got him."

"Then *I* come to the rescue. That sounds better."

Pat frowned. "It'll be hard work. You can't let them into the garden. They'll only find their way back to the loft again."

"That's okay. I'll take them to the woods and free them there."

"If you don't mind traipsing half a mile every morning. Don't expect any help from me. I've got other things to do. This is *your* job."

He stepped into the passage. "I'd better get rid of those chocolates. They won't be any good now."

"No. Leave them." I followed him out. "There are bits the mice haven't got at: Santa's feet, for example. I'm not dumping anything until I've inspected it."

He shook his head. "You're mad. They'll be full of germs, even mouse-droppings, I shouldn't wonder. I'm dumping them."

My heart sank, but the thought of mouse-droppings did take the edge off my appetite.

"It's a crazy idea anyway, storing your Christmas chocolates in the loft. They were bound to attract mice."

I watched him climb the loft-ladder while I stood forlornly at the bottom, thinking of my chocolate feast, or what was left of it, being flung without mercy into the bin.

"You'd better keep *some*," I called up, "to put in the mouse-trap."

Pat bought the trap later that day. "It's very small," I said. "Not much room for a mouse to move about in."

I found a transparent box, three times the size of the trap, with air-holes in it. I'll transfer each mouse into that, I thought. There'll be more room. Then I'll take it to the woods and let it out.

That night, Pat took the trap to the loft and put some chocolate in it. The next morning when I went up to investigate, I found a small brown mouse sitting inside, a look of surprise on its face.

I felt a flutter of nervousness as I picked up the trap. I'd never seen a mouse up close before. I took it downstairs and put it carefully on the kitchen table. I felt sorry for the poor little thing. It was anxious to get out and trying to climb the transparent walls. I opened the trap and dropped the mouse carefully into the box lying beside it. It sniffed around for a bit, then began to wash its face.

"Come on, I'll give you a lift to the woods," Pat said, his face appearing round the corner of the kitchen. "But don't expect it every morning. About time you learnt to drive."

When we arrived at the fringe of the woods, I lay the box on the grass, and opened it up.

The mouse peered around him cautiously, seeming in no hurry to go. At last, he placed his front paws at the top edge of the box and peeped over. Finally, he jumped out and scampered away till all you could see was the whisk of his tail.

Every morning, it was the same routine: the climb to the loft to find the trapped mouse, its passage from trap to box, the walk to the woods, its final run through the grass. I grew quite fond of the creatures. "They're not dirty" I told Patrick. "Look how they wash themselves: the backs of their necks, behind their ears." One little mouse let me stroke its head while it washed. It felt soft, delicate. I stopped worrying about their long tails and pointy faces. "They're pretty," I said.

"They might be pretty," Pat grumbled, "but they harbour germs. I don't want germs everywhere, thank you. We should have got the council in. God knows how many more mice are up there."

Freud would have found my husband an interesting case. He's obsessed about germs. If a can falls out of the fridge, he'll wash it before putting it back. And if he offers to do the dishes, he sees they're thoroughly washed by hand first, before being popped in the dishwasher.

You can guess, therefore, what a flap I was in when, one morning, an unusually clever and athletic little mouse refused to be dispatched from the trap to the box but leapt down to the floor instead. He scuttled all over the kitchen looking for a way out. I tried to catch him but no such luck. He vanished behind one of the units and wouldn't come out again.

Pat threw a fit at the news. "You see. What did I tell you? I knew something like this would happen." He flung up his arms. "It was stark staring mad, dropping a mouse from a trap into a box."

He removed the trap from the loft, put some chocolate in it and placed it behind the wall-unit nearest the kitchen door.

That night, taking a peep in the trap, I found that the chocolate had gone. So had the mouse.

"That's one clever mouse," I exclaimed.

Tight-lipped, Pat adjusted the spring of the trap, put in more chocolate, and placed it behind the unit again.

The same thing happened. In the morning, the chocolate was gone, along with the mouse.

"It's a Mensa mouse," I gasped.

"Mensa nothing. It's that flaming trap. It's useless." He flung it in the bin in disgust. "I'll get a new one."

I felt sad to find the plucky little mouse imprisoned in the new trap the following morning. When I looked at him sitting forlornly in his glass prison, he turned away and hurriedly washed his face. Perhaps he was embarrassed at having been caught.

That morning I took him, still in his trap, into the woods. This time Pat drove me there. He wanted to make sure that it was the last he'd see of this bold mouse.

We kept the new trap in the loft for the next few days, but no more mice got caught in it. Perhaps they'd moved out. I was relieved. Pat had threatened to call the council.

However, the day before Christmas, I came across something else there. A mass of white stuff spilling out of a dust bag which I'd thought was full of old toys.

I pulled it out. It was the white coat I'd come up to find in the first place – at least, what was left of it, after those hungry mice. Leather and fur had been nibbled away. It wasn't even fit for a jumble-sale.

Sadly, I held out the remains and scanned them.

I must have been crazy to imagine it would still fit me, even as a jacket. Had I really been that slim forty years ago?

I carried it down the loft ladder, to shove in the bin. Perhaps the mice had done me a favour, I thought. They'd found my coat, reminding me how much weight I'd put on over the years. And they'd stolen my chocolates, helping me start on my new year's resolution.

But it's not the New Year yet and I'm off to do some last minute Christmas shopping. I shan't go mad, but I'm a strong believer in the old saying: *A little of what you fancy does you good.*

HAITIAN RITUAL – 1981

It's startling how swift and sudden night falls in Haiti. It drops like a black curtain, shutting out all signs of life.

I feel a crease of anxiety forming between my eyes. Where the hell are we?

I lean forward in the taxi. "Are you sure we're on the right road, Pierre? We must have reached the place by this time?"

Our driver laughs. "Don't worry, Madame. I not lose the way. We arrive soon. Only a few kilometres. Okay?"

My husband, Patrick, sighs, "He told us that half an hour ago."

I'm growing uneasy. We seem to have driven for miles in the setting sun, along the bumpy roads of Haiti, and way past Port au Prince. We've covered remote villages, hills and barren plains. Now, in the darkness, it's hard to tell where we are. At this moment, we seem to be driving into a forest.

I nudge Patrick. "Let's go back."

I sense his lips tightening in the darkness, the stubborn gleam in his eyes. "Forget it. This was *your* idea, not mine. We're not turning back now, not when we've got this far."

Waste of time trying to melt him. He's been cross with me all day because of this trip.

"You just don't *think*, do you?" he grumbles. "You go ahead and arrange things, without even bothering to consult me. What I wanted was to do something normal for a change. Like go out to dinner."

Pierre must have heard us bickering. He ground the car to a halt. The light went on. He turned round to face us.

"Be calm, Madame. You will enjoy it. There will be dancing and singing. It will be – how you say? – the bright light of your vacation. Okay?" He opens the car-door, his face beaming with enthusiasm. "Me. I will enjoy it also." He jumps out. "Come. We arrive."

What? Here?

We clamber out, glancing around us. We are in some sort of clearing, surrounded by trees. From the light of the moon breaking through the clouds, we see at the far end, a raised courtyard or stage with a ceremonial altar at the back. It looks like a temple. In front is a scattering of chairs.

Even though he's mad at me, Patrick grasps my hand and squeezes it. We follow Pierre to the courtyard and take two of the chairs to sit on. Pierre sits on another.

I am chewing at my fingers, still wishing we hadn't come. But it's too late now. In this solitary shanty-town at the edge of the forest, we are far from the lights of Port au Prince. There's no going back. Patrick, I know, will not be persuaded. As for our driver, he cannot wait for the thing to begin.

We sit silent in the darkness, watching and waiting.

Before us is the temple, pillared, roofed and empty.

And out of the stillness, from behind it, comes the croaking of a thousand frogs, harsh and unceasing.

Patrick presses my hand, anxious to comfort me.

"Not long now," Pierre tells us. "Soon they'll light up the temple, and it will start."

I let out a deep breath. We'll have to see it through to the end. It will be only polite. But already, I feel queasy. Annoyed with myself too. For I realise now that my husband was right. About everything.

It was I who had wanted to come, threatening to go alone, if he wouldn't come with me. In my ignorance, I'd expected a short drive to some lush hotel where we'd see dancing girls going into trances to the sound of Voodoo drums. An imitation of the real thing, something to entertain the tourists - such tourists as existed. Our own hotel was empty apart from ourselves and a couple of Americans.

We chatted with one of them tonight while waiting for Pierre. He was quick to confirm Pat's fears about the entertainment I'd arranged. "I doubt if it's a floor show," he said, with a chuckle, "or some fake ritual. But everyone to his taste, I guess."

A tremor of dismay rose to my throat. I shook it off. It's an assumption, I told myself, not fact.

So far, Pierre has not let us down. We enjoyed our trip to Kenscoff up in the mountains to visit the Friday market, our drive through the main streets of the capital, to see its art galleries and restaurants. We've had glimpses of the Tonton Macoute, of course, the president's loyal and sinister militia men. Pierre tells us that the name in English is `Mr Knapsack'. It stems from an African legend in which a scary old man grabbed children unawares and carried them off in his sack. From what I've heard of the Tonton Macoute, it's an apt name.

And tonight, on the way here, Pierre has shown us the rest of Port au Prince, eager to point out prisons and palaces, a famous brothel, and, of course, the presidential building of Baby Doc. We've seen grimmer sights: a legless man, crossing the road, like a crab, with the help of his hands; barefoot children rummaging in the dirt.

Leaving the capital, we've passed through squalid shanty-towns. Then on and on through bare darkness, where poverty is sensed rather than seen. No hotels now. No music. Nothing except the chorus of frogs and the occasional screech of a cockerel.

A stirring from behind the courtyard, amongst the trees, forces me back to the present. There are beams of torchlight, a murmur of voices, then footsteps coming closer in an even stride. Soon a massive woman, turbaned, and dark as the night, strides up the steps and onto the courtyard. She is bedecked with candles.

"That's the Mambo," Pierre whispers.

She sets up the candles, arranges them into groups and lights them one by one, slowly and carefully. After that, she kneels down and, in the flickering light, chalks upon the floor the required signs and symbols in preparation for the ceremony.

Having performed these initial rites, she stands up again, moves back, and disappears into the darkness. Later, she will return with her offering to the gods.

Now the Voodoo drums begin to beat. A shrill chanting breaks out. And devotees of the Voodoo faith snake their way to the candlelit floor, moving and singing in rhythm to the drum-beat.

The ritual dance has begun.

The music is monotonous, but hypnotic. There are three drums. The largest is called the mamman. The leader-drummer beats this fiercely with one stick and a hand. The smaller drums give out hypnotic counter-rhythms. The drums are for summoning the spirits to come and possess the performers' bodies. Each spirit is appealed to with the same song and dance three times.

Once the music starts the mambo takes a kind of rattle from the ceremonial altar and joins the others in the dancing and singing of ritual songs.

The songs, like the drum-beats, are hypnotic, the voices piercing. The dancers are tireless. On and on they go, like bright, tropical birds flitting across the stage until, one after another, with mounting excitement, they fall into a trance.

The whole thing fascinates and horrifies both at once. What I find troubling is the end of the dance with the impending sacrifice. And that end is approaching.

Soon I see a young man fetch a chicken on to the stage. The poor thing looks half-dead already. He swings it backwards and forwards as he dances round and round on the temple floor.

This is the bit I was dreading. Neither Patrick nor I can bear to see violence to animals. Yet we are prepared to eat meat, so what are we but hypocrites?

Nevertheless, I have to close my eyes to shut out the sight. It makes little difference. I can guess what is happening. The man is killing the chicken, biting through its neck until it's dead. The chicken lets out not a single squawk.

This marks the end of the ritual.

There is an outburst of appreciative shouts and claps from Pierre, and some gentler clapping from me and Patrick in a show of politeness.

We rise slowly and soon we are hobbling along behind Pierre to his taxi. It's late and we're half asleep. As Pierre drives us back to our hotel, I fall into an uneasy doze. I see again the young man dancing round the stage with the sacrificial chicken. Only this time, *I* am the chicken. I feel helpless and giddy as I'm swung backwards and forwards and round and round. Suddenly, the dancer stops. I see his jaws open and a set of gleaming white teeth ready to strike at my neck ...

I wake with a jump.

As we drive on, I try to rationalise the ritual killing of the bird. It is, I'm told, a humane way of despatching an animal. Maybe. I doubt, anyway, if the sacrificial chickens here are any worse off than the battery hens we have at home.

We are nearing the end of our journey now. Pat is getting hungry. It's a long time since we've eaten. I expect we'll have a snack at the hotel before we go to bed. Some sandwiches perhaps.

Hopefully, not chicken.

DRESSED FOR THE OCCASION

It had been a bad move. I knew that from the start. But Pat was impulsive. If, all of a sudden, there was something he wanted to do, and a chance to do it, then do it he would. No stopping to consider if we were suitably prepared. Or bothering about the possible consequences.

That's how we came to be sitting in the little red sailing-boat, drifting further and further away from the shores of Jamaica. My husband, dressed in his new tropical suit, was busy attending to the sail. I, clutching my sun-hat with one hand, my precious handbag with the other, was trying to maintain the boat's balance by constantly changing my sitting position. That's when I wasn't ducking my head to avoid being struck by the boom.

"Look over there!" Pat said, suddenly, screwing up his eyes and peering into the distance. "I think it's a desert island."

I followed his gaze and gave a dismissive laugh. "Looks more like a rock to me."

My husband is mad about desert islands. For him, a place empty of people meant peace and quiet and a chance to enjoy the wonders of nature.

"We can soon find out," he said. "It's not that far. Let's make for it. It'll be easy."

It wasn't easy.

The trouble started when we sailed into a rough patch of water where gentle little waves gave way to big bold ones. They slapped aggressively against the sides of the boat and sometimes spat into it.

I had to keep really busy, shifting my weight from one side of the boat to the other in my effort to keep it steady. Pat, a worried frown on his face now, promptly forgot about desert islands and was trying to turn it round so we could make for the shore again.

But the boat was unpredictable and didn't seem to want to turn round. It was I who got the blame.

"Isn't it about time you did your share of the work?" Pat demanded, glaring at me. "It's obvious you're more interested in that handbag and all your other trivia, than in doing your bit to keep us afloat."

"Well, I like that!" Flames of indignation shot up inside me. "We'd both be overboard by now, if it wasn't for me." I was about to give him another mouthful, when the boom gave me a whack across the head.

I swore at it, furious, forgetting for a moment my job of keeping the boat the right way up. It was at that moment that the bow rose from the water and I found myself sitting below in the stern. We were about to capsize.

There was an ominous splash. A second later, Pat was nowhere to be seen.

Still clutching my handbag, I threw my weight towards the toppling bow. Instantly, it dropped, and the boat was level again.

But where was Pat?

My heart began to pound.

There was a splashing and a floundering nearby. Suddenly, an arm appeared above the waves. A grim face followed. I let out a gasp of relief and held out a helpful arm. He ignored it, and dragged himself over the stern. I raced to the bow and sat down hard.

Pat, coughing and spluttering, was dripping seawater from his sad, tropical suit. It was clear he'd never be able to wear it again. On top of everything else, he had lost a shoe.

Tight-lipped, he ignored such trivia, focussing his whole attention on turning the boat into calm waters. This time he managed it, and soon we were sailing for the shore again.

"If you'd been concentrating more on the boat, and less on your handbag and that ridiculous sun-hat, we'd have been all right," he growled.

I suggested, unnecessarily perhaps, that next time we went sailing, we would dress for the occasion and leave behind air-tickets, dollars, travellers cheques, camera and other such trivia I kept in my handbag.

"How was I to know you were going to hire a boat?" I demanded.

Pat, still wet and minus a shoe, said nothing. But if looks could have killed …

Lightning Source UK Ltd.
Milton Keynes UK
UKHW040954271122
412909UK00001B/57